I0547345

ARCHIE

Sheppard's Shadow Book 2

KATHI S. BARTON

This is a work of fiction. Names, characters, places, and incidents are products of the author's imagination or are used fictitiously and are not to be construed as real. Any resemblance to actual events, locations, organizations, or persons, living or dead, is entirely coincidental.

World Castle Publishing, LLC
Pensacola, Florida
Copyright © 2024 Kathi S. Barton
Paperback ISBN: 9798891262447
eBook ISBN: 9798891262454
First Edition World Castle Publishing, LLC, July 15, 2024
http://www.worldcastlepublishing.com
Licensing Notes
All rights reserved. No part of this book may be used or reproduced in any manner whatsoever without written permission, except in the case of brief quotations embodied in articles and reviews.
Cover: Cover Designs by Karen
Cover-designs-by-karen.com
Editor: Karen Fuller

Chapter 1

When Archie had gone to the salad bar twice more after ordering his pizza, he came back to his table to find Nash sitting at his table. Not bothering with asking him, his younger brother, what he wanted, he watched as he got up and made himself a huge meat-only salad, too. As soon as the waitress brought him his pizza, Nash took two slices for himself and rolled them into a long tube, eating them nearly in one bite.

"You're paying for dinner. I hope you know that." Nash nodded, saying that they'd talk about it. "Why are you bothering me here? I was having a good day until you showed up. That's not entirely true. I'm treating myself after helping a young man not end up in jail. Where is Sunny, anyway?

I have a feeling she'd not be too thrilled about you taking my meal. She likes me."

"Yeah? Well, she loves me, and I get to have sex with her. A lot of it. All over the house, too. In the bathroom. On the counters. On my favorite chair. Which, I might point out, is my doubly favorite chair now. " Rolling his eyes at his brother, he asked him what he was doing here. "I have some questions for you. I don't know that you'll have all the answers, but they're important that I voice them not get answers for them necessarily. Also, I have a lot of things to talk to you about. Some of it's good, and the rest? I guess we'll find out how you like it. This is really good. I've not had a salad in years, I don't think."

"Technically, you're not having one now. It's mostly meat and cheese, like a sub without the bun. All right, you want to talk, then talk. But you're still paying for my dinner." Waving him off, Archie had a feeling that he was going to leave him with the bill. Not that he really minded but it was the principal of the thing. He'd really been having a good day until then. "What did you want to know?"

"First, and this shouldn't be a surprise to

you, Josiha stepped down from his position as leap leader just about an hour ago. His plan is going to be to hang out at the offices for you to shadow until *you* take over. I hadn't any idea that it was a done deal for you to be taking over. Also, you should know that once you take over and are comfy with the position, he'll be gone. I didn't dig too deeply into that, but knowing that he won't come back on you is great news, don't you think?" He said that he'd not known that either. "You should go by there soon and have a talk with him. Sunny said to tell you not to go alone, either. For you to take me. Again, I don't know if he'll give you any shit, but she wants to protect you, so I'd let her if I were you."

"I can do that. What else?" He told him the second part as the waitress came to the table. After ordering another pizza for them, Archie had to think about why Nash thought he needed to take the job. "Who cares who runs the shadow? I mean, I guess I could do it. However, I'd be a bit more present than Joshia ever was. Not to say that I'm taking it but he's been lax for a long time. I don't want something like this to consume my life. I want to have one. I started to say again, but I've never had a life that didn't involve what Mother told us to do any more than the rest of you did."

He was so happy that his mother was dead along with her father that he was sleeping better at night. She had pitted them against one another their whole lives so that they hated to be around one another. Then Sunny, Nash's mate, had come into their lives and it was as if they'd had their eyes opened for the first time. She didn't even have to point things out to them anymore to have them see what a shitty and painfully terrible life they'd had. It was all their plans to now have a life. Not necessarily a happy one, he knew that would be easy to have, but a productive one too. And he also got to hang out with his brothers more. He loved them with all his heart.

"He has." He had to think about what his brother was answering him about when he realized they were still talking about the leap. "I talked with Lily this morning. Did you know that if you take over the shadow, you become an immortal? Lily seems to think that he's been at it for so long. He was just doing his time. Bored, she thought that he had seen too much and was bored out of his mind with the shit, so he just ignored it. Not a good way to run a leap, but that's what she told me." Archie could see that, too. It was why he decided that he was going to go to college and try something else. Anything else that would stimulate his mind and body. "Also, Lily said that as soon as you take it, she seems to think that it's a foregone conclusion that you will take it, you'll get a shit ton of power. I don't know what that might entail but she told me that you need to be with people in the event that it puts you down for a while. I would count on that. It's been pointed out to me that with great power comes exhaustion." His brother laughed.

"Good to know. Though again, I don't know that I'd take the job. As I said this morning, I want to be able to live a life that I've never had before." Nash nodded but didn't comment. "What else? You said several things."

"You are aware that Lily is the Queen of the Earth, right? I want to make sure you understand… When Lily acknowledges that Sunny is her daughter, we'll get a lot of power, a great deal of it. I was told that the family will get it as well. While I have an idea that it will make us powerful, I don't have a lot of details about what that might mean for us. I could have asked her, but she was upset with me already. I really love to piss her off a little. She's adorable when she's mad at me." Rolling his eyes and nodding again, he ate the last slice of his pizza. The second one was coming toward them even as he realized that he was still really hungry. "Also, and this one boggles my mind to no end. We'll have an endless supply of funds. I had to ask because — well, endless? What the hell does that even mean? Anyway, we'll get that as soon as she does her thing with my mate. I'm thinking that they might mean like power funds. At least, that's what I keep telling myself. I don't want to think beyond that for now."

"Endless, huh? And I completely understand about it being something that would be scary. One's endless supply of money could mean different things to different people, I suppose, too. Well, I guess that would be nice to be able to help out the shadow if there is enough left over after we pay some bills. I know it's not all that big of one. The leap, I mean. I think that Joshia said that it was less than fifty cats. With us included." Nash told him that there was a great deal of money already in the coffers for the shadow that hadn't been touched in decades. He'd just been too lazy to do anything with that. "What the fuck? You mean that there could have been all these improvements, and he just sat on it not doing a thing? Christ, no wonder there are only fifty people in the shadow. No one is getting help, so they just went to greener pastures. Anything else I need to be made aware of?"

"Yes, plenty." When he didn't say anything more, Archie looked at his brother. He seemed to be lost in thought, and he found himself reaching beyond where they were to see if he could figure anything out. "Archie, do you trust me?"

"With all that I am." And in that moment, he truly did believe that. Also that he'd lay down his life for his brother, any one of them. "What's going on, Nash?" He leaned toward him, which surprised him that he was speaking rather than using their link if he wanted it to be a secret. "Nash, you're scaring me a little. Actually, a great deal."

"The three people over there at the booth just to the right of the front counter are planning to rob the place. The manager knows about it. She's in over her head with owing them a great deal of money from her brother's debt. She's going to be hurt badly while the rest of us will be put to death. Not you and I, but everyone else," Archie asked if they were planning to hurt anyone in the back room, too. "Yes. All of us. I need you to take my hand, Archie. Just for a second so that I can protect us both."

He didn't hesitate at all but put his hand out so that Nash could do whatever was necessary to keep them safe. The brush of his hand over his was warm but he could feel whatever he gave him start to heat up his hand then up and over his body. It was beginning to be too warm when a wave of something…powerful washed over him.

"Archie, don't pass out on me. Come on now. You got this." Shaking his head, Archie said that he was a little dizzy. "Dizzy is better than dead. Just follow my lead, and we'll get everyone out of here in one piece. All right?"

"Yes. Do whatever you need." When Nash stood up, so did Archie. He wasn't as dizzy as he'd been at first but his body was beginning to hum with whatever Nash had done to him. He thought that 'hum' was the perfect word for what he was feeling. Not bad, just humming along. When Nash headed for the three people in the corner, he told him to go to the back room and help the manager. He was nearly back there when he heard the sound of one pissed-off cat then nothing at all.

"You can't be back here." Archie told the man making pizzas that the place was about to be robbed and that he needed for him to get out. "Just fucking great. I've had it up to here with this place. All right. I'm done here. This is the fourth time this place has been hit in a year. I'm not coming back."

The man tossed his apron onto the half-finished pizza he'd been making and left by the back door. Alarms were still going off when Archie entered the office of the manager. The woman was sitting there with a gun to her mouth. Sitting down trying to remain calm, she stared at him with her eyes full of falling tears. She pulled the gun out of her mouth long enough to tell him to go away.

"I can't do that, I'm afraid. Not and be able to live with myself knowing that you were going to kill yourself. Please don't do whatever you're thinking of doing." She said that she didn't want to go to prison for someone else's trouble. The gun was still in her hand, but it was no longer in her mouth, for which he was thankful. "No, I can see that. Where is your brother while you're dealing with this shit here?"

"Dead. He decided to get himself killed and

leave me hanging. I don't even know how they figured out that I was related to the fucking bastard, but since he's been dead, they've been showing up here or at my house demanding money. Wait, how did you know I had a brother? Who's been talking to you?" Archie told her that he had read her mind. Then he asked her why she thought that killing herself was going to help. "Great. A loony reading my mind. And it won't solve anything, but I won't have to deal with it either. I'm sick of being the one that has people dumping their—you know, I'm not even supposed to be managing this place. I'm just a waitress who started helping out the real manager when she was too drunk to care what happened here on a daily basis. Since I like to have a check and food in my belly, I took over. Of course, no one is happy about it but at least the employees are getting their checks on time. This is just bullshit."

"It would drive me crazy too. But not to the point where you are now. But then I have a feeling that I don't know everything. I think this, not the gun part but what you're doing, that's commendable of you. Brave too. Where is the manager right now?" She told him she didn't know, but she thought that she came in to take the deposits to the bank at night. "No doubt after you're closed. Are you sure that the money is getting to the bank?"

"No. And again, I don't care all that much. I have the money witnessed by an off-duty cop before I put it in the bank bag and leave it in the safe for the day. I don't have the authorization to deposit money. The cop records it all for me, and then I email it to corporate and to both him and myself. I might be a waitress, but I know how to cover my ass when I need to. I've certainly have had enough practice at it. Except for my brother's crap." He grinned at her, and she cocked a brow at him. "I don't know what you think might be funny, mister, but I have shit going on, and you're not helping me get to the end."

"My brother, you've not met him as yet, but he's taken care of the problem in the lobby for you. I don't know what he did—I know that I would have killed them, but then Nash has a better head on his shoulders than I do most of the time. By the way, my name is Archibald Sheppard. I go by Archie. You're Carrie. Your nametag gives you away. But back to my brother. Which isn't to say that he might have killed them already, but there you have it." She asked him to get out of her office. "Sure. But in the meantime, you do want to have dinner with me tonight?"

"No. Now, leave me alone. I'm sick of this world and those people like the ones in the lobby. Yes, I know who they are and what they want. And I'm sick of rolling over for men. I won't be able to do that again if I'm gone." He hoped that he had given her enough that she'd put the gun down. At least it wasn't pointed at her anymore.

He did leave her, but he wasn't sure that he'd be staying away. She was a spitfire, and he wanted to get to know her. Before he was to the dining area again, it hit him like a ton of bricks. He'd just met his mate. Turning to go back and talk to her more, he heard the sound of a gunshot before he reached her office.

"Christ."

~*~

While riding to the hospital in the back of the ambulance, Carrie decided that she was going to make sure that when she got out of there, she was going to find a place to hide and do what she had tried to do earlier. She didn't even know how she missed. She put the gun near her forehead, fired, and the next thing she knew, she was where she was right now. In the back of an ambulance…alive.

"I'm afraid that it won't do you any good. I have your scent, and since I gave you a bit of my blood, actually quite a bit of it, you can't hide your feelings from me either. And because I had to give you a bit of my blood to save you, I'll have a firsthand look at your emotions, too. I know you really wanted to die, Carrie. But I couldn't allow that. I'm so very sorry. But I need you around. By the way, I never got your last name." Glaring at the man had him laughing. *"You're not having a good time? I believe that I am. You're also going to love my family."* And why could she suddenly talk to the loony cake this way? He told her. She no more believed that than she did that he'd given her his blood. That was just…it was gross. She didn't even want to think about how he'd done that either.

"Are they as nutty as you are?" He laughed harder when she told him she hated him. And while she'd only just met the man, she had a feeling that his life up until recently hadn't been the best. *"What's happened to you? Did someone shit in your oats or something? No, that can't be right. You're a cat. It's doubtful that you've ever eaten anything as cheap*

as oatmeal."

"As a matter of fact, I love oats. As for something shitting in them, no, it's not happening anymore. You see, my mother recently passed on along with her father. I'm happy about that. Now, while I know that sounds like I'm a bastard of a son, it's not true. I'm actually just figuring out that I'm a nice enough sort of person. I have lived a sheltered life, thanks to my mother controlling every aspect of my life, but myself and my brothers are working things out." She asked him if he meant LouCinda Sheppard. *"Yes. I'm sure that you read about it in the paper. It was written about all over the world, I was told. Her father wasn't all that much better than his daughter. But while it hurts me that I didn't have a good relationship with her, I am glad that they're both gone. The two of them killed a lot of people before they were killed."*

"I'm sorry about that. I read about the trial not ending well. And a lot of people are left to wonder if their missing family members were part of her killing spree." He said that the attorneys were taking care that everyone they had records of have been notified. *"Good."*

They were just pulling up in front of the hospital when she was told to please keep her head down. There were reporters all over the entrance, and they were going to bring her in through the emergency department. Not around back where ambulances usually did their drop-offs.

With the blanket over her head, she could hear everything that was going on. There must have been a couple of reporters in the ED because she heard someone telling them to leave or be arrested. Not paying attention to whether or not they left, she was amazed at how wonderful it felt to have her hand held by Mr. Sheppard. Trying to pull away from him didn't work, so she made herself leave her hand limp in his much larger one. His laughter pissed her off.

"You are going to be a handful, aren't you? All right, you can remove the covering. We're in a room." She wanted to know why she was even in here when she looked down at her blouse as they sat her up on the other bed. There was a great deal of blood, too, and she had to put her head back when it occurred to her that it was all hers. "Steady now. You don't want to pass out on me now. Breathe in and—"

"I know how to breathe." But she did listen to his instructions so that she wouldn't pass out.

"There is no telling what you'd have them do to me if I were to faint. Why are you even following me around? Don't you have widows to toss out of their homes or something?"

"Why do people think that first thing? I mean, sure, I have some money, but I've never once even been tempted to toss anyone out on their ass. That's not true. I did toss my mother and grandfather out before they were killed. I might toss you around just to see if your bosom bounces as well as I think they might. Will they?" She could only stare at him, not sure what to say. "Close your mouth, dear. The doctor wants to talk to you."

She didn't hear a single word that the doctor said to her. Carrie was still trying to figure out why he'd brought up her breasts right now. When the doctor left her, she looked around the room and wondered yet again why she was there.

"You have a broken collar bone as well as some contusions along your cheeks, lovely as they are, that need to be stitched up. And just so you know, you've single-handedly stopped the restaurant from being robbed by taking out the three men who came there to do the job." She asked them how he had come to that conclusion.

"Oh, that's not what happened. It's just what the police and the reporters think happened. Lily broke your collarbone when she slapped the gun out of your hand. The rest is what they saw when they got there."

"Who is Lily?" He told her something about a queen and earth. "I'm sorry. What? I mean, did you just tell me that Lily is the queen of the earth who kept me alive and that she's been keeping an eye on me for you? I don't know that I'm all that happy with that. I mean, she could have kept a better eye on me than she had, don't you think? I've been beaten nearly to death, stabbed, shot—not by me those times, and I've been thrown—why are you looking all fuzzy?"

"My cat doesn't care for the fact that you've been hurt. He's showing you how upset he is. And I want to find these men and teach them a lesson in treating my mate." She turned her head away so that he would not see her pain. "Carrie? I'm sorry, honey. I didn't mean to upset you."

"Okay, first of all. I'm not upset. Hurt? Yes. But not upset. Also, I can't be your mate. Well, I suppose that I could be, but I don't want to be. You do not want to saddle yourself with a woman who is in debt for thousands upon thousands of dollars because her brother is a fucking deadbeat that...did you tell me that your cat was upset?" He nodded and told her that he was a jaguar. "A jaguar. You're a jaguar."

"Yes. Not only that but I might be the leap leader. Which would make you the female version of myself. Gives you lots of power, too." She glared at him. "Honey, I don't know if you're aware of this or not but I think you're just too adorable to be upset with when you get all mean looking at me. It just occurred to me what my brother meant when he said he liked to piss off his mate. Sunny is scary, but she loves us all."

"You're insane." He thanked her. "No, it's not a compliment. It's...do you have any idea how that sounds? That you're a shifter? I mean, don't get me wrong. If you believe it, then I will, too. But there are—what the fuck did you do?"

"I've become my cat for you. I must tell you that he's happy to be with you." She backed as far as she could from the gianormace cat that was standing next to her bed. Reaching for the call cord to get someone to come and save her, the furry fuzz ball leaped up on the bed and licked her face. *"He loves*

you too."

"No one loves me." He told her that he did, and the big cat licked her face again. She noticed that he'd not touched the side of her face where she was cut up. When he leaped off the bed and became Archie again, she felt disappointment all the way to her toes. Then the door opened. There stood three men that could have been the man that had just been a— "If you tell me that you're cats, too, then I'm going to have them ship me off to la-la land. Brothers, right?"

"Yes. Archie is the oldest. I'm Nash. My name is Nashville but I decided that I like Nash better. This is our younger brothers Weston and Beau. You're Carrie Hunter Sheppard." She said that she knew who she was and she was not Sheppard. "I hate to break it to you, but that's what the newspapers are calling you. That might be better, to be honest. You're protected by magic, as well as all of us."

"Just how many are there of you? And so, you know, you look like you've been cut from the same mold." He thanked her. "Why is it impossible to say something to you guys, and you think it's a compliment?"

"Because no one has ever been nice to us before." That hurt her not just in her heart but in her very soul. She told them that she was sorry. "No worries, honey. You're with us now, so I'm thinking that we're going to start having a better life. I know that I am. My mate, Sunny, is everything to me. Just as you are to Archie."

"I've only just met him." The nurse came in and told her that she was going to go to preop. Nervous all of a sudden, she felt herself suddenly relax when Archie took her hand into his. It wasn't a habit that she wanted to keep, but it was nice to know that he was going to be there for her. Why? She didn't know, but she knew on some level that he would be forever.

They rolled her down to the preop room, and she was glad again that Archie was with her. He had an effect on her nerves that made her feel like she was going to be all right. Again, she didn't understand that, but she was glad for it. As soon as they gave her something to relax her, Carrie was drifting off. She was sure that she'd not said anything aloud, but she told Archie that she loved him. She was being silly, she knew. But she really thought that she knew what her heart was telling her.

"Hello there." She had to take a few minutes to get her eyes to focus and saw that another brother was sitting in the chair next to her bed. She asked him who he was. Or she thought that she did. "You did. However, you didn't ask it out loud. I'm sorry, but I didn't want you to hurt when you spoke. You've been out for a few days. My name is Wrangler. As you've guessed, yes, I am one of the brothers of Archie. I'm the third born. Can I get you anything? They said that you shouldn't allow the pain to get too much for you. That if you need something, ask for it sooner rather than later."

"Am I going to be all right?" He told her that she had some stitches that were in her arm and that they'd not known she'd been hurt there until they got her in the operating room. *"Why haven't I healed up? I mean, that's what is supposed to happen, right? I don't know if I believe all the stuff I've read about shifters. But that is constant in all the books I read."*

"Yes, well, you've not said that you accept Archie. He's claimed you, not in a bad way, but just telling everyone that you're his mate. In order to heal, and just so you don't do that immediately, the police have yet to speak to you and you have to make it look good for the public. They get kind of testy when people heal too quickly." She said she understood. "Good. He just said that he claimed you as his mate. And being that he's holding off accepting the position of leap leader until he can speak to you about it, he went to Joshia and told him. That's all you need to do."

"Sounds too easy." He said that it wasn't really. *"What's going to happen when I say those words? I immediately heal or something? And what happens to me when I do? I'm assuming that I'm going to heal from what you're saying."*

"You will heal completely. Even the things that haven't been known to you as yet will disappear. I'm only telling you this so you understand what will happen to you. You have several spots of cancer in your left breast. It's not bad yet, but it would have eventually taken you. I'm sorry. I'm not known for my tact." She told him that she wouldn't have it any other way. "Good. There is more, but I think your pain is getting the better of you. Before my brother comes in here and beats me up for keeping you from your pain meds, please call the nurse for something. Please?"

She nodded, just realizing that he was right. She was hurting. He had to help her with the button and the nurse came in immediately to give her meds. Wrangler didn't leave her, even holding her hand while the meds took her under. She didn't understand her need for Archie just then, but she closed her eyes and allowed the medication to take her under.

Chapter 2

"Did you see this? It says that your sister is a hero. It says her name is Sheppard now. When did she marry, and why wasn't it in the paper or something? I'm assuming that this is bullshit. She's about the stupidest person that I've ever met." Doug took the newspaper from Shelly and read the headline. "What did I tell you about jerking shit from me, Douglas? I will hand you things, but you're not to take them because you want them. It's considered rude and uncouth." Doug ignored Shelly for the moment.

He was sick to death of her whining about her own set of rules about shit. Trying to read the paper while ignoring her, she snatched the paper from him, ripping the paper in half and destroying his barely-held temper. Not that he had a good hold on it most of the time, but she was on his last nerve today. A quick, hard slap to her face had her falling backward and ripping the paper in half. Christ, his temper exploded, and he felt it right behind his eyes all the way to his feet. It just took him over the edge.

Picking her up by her hair, he slapped her several times until he had to rein in his anger or kill her. As much as he wanted her dead, he needed her, too. Dropping her to the floor, he picked up the other half of the paper and noticed that the article that he had been reading wasn't affected by her stupidity. Sitting at the little table that came with the hotel that they'd been renting, he spread out the paper and decided that he was going to have to do something to make it up to Shelly, or she'd not leave him alone. He could almost feel her pestering her hourly until he did lose it again. Christ, didn't she ever learn?

The paper read like a blow-by-blow accounting of what had happened when the men that he'd hired had gone to collect the money that she'd had. While he knew that she didn't make all that much, he also knew that the restaurant was insured and that all that they took to pay off his debt would be covered. Why more people didn't take advantage of this way to make ends meet was beyond him. It wasn't all that hard. Well, not normally. He had no idea why his sister had stepped in this time. The stupid bitch.

Actually, Douglas knew that his sister was far from stupid. The bitch part was true, but not her being stupid. When they'd been kids together, she would always make great grades when he nearly failed each and every test he took. Mostly, it was because he didn't try all that hard. And she worked herself to death just to keep herself from getting anything lower than an A. Then, when she'd gotten accepted into college at the age of sixteen, he'd made fun of her relentlessly until she moved away.

Their parents never had much to do with them as children, either. No matter how hard Carrie tried to show them her grade cards or a test she would have aced, they simply ignored her. Him, too, for the most part. The only time they noticed him was when he'd been arrested for something or when he fucked up bad enough that it required them to pay for an attorney. The older he got, the more frequent that happened. Until they passed away.

To this day, he still had no idea what they died of. First, his mom got really sick, ending up in the hospital, and then his dad. A week after Mom passed away, Dad died in his sleep. He'd been so angry with them that he'd not ever been able to forgive them. To leave him all alone after Carrie had left him as well. People were just asses, and he couldn't stand to be around them much anymore, either.

"You fucking hit me." Douglas looked at Shelly and noticed something that he'd not before. She had aged a great deal since he'd first met her. Christ he realized, that had been nearly fifteen years ago now. Reaching out to touch the streak of gray that was getting fairly wide on her head, she smacked his hand away. Smacking her back, he yanked on a handful of her hair until he held onto the hank of hair that had been on her head. "What the fuck did you do? Christ, Douglas, that fucking hurt. I think you snatched me about bawld."

"I was taking out the gray. I don't like it." He turned his back to her but listened carefully for her to move. She didn't care for anyone to turn their back on her any more than he did when someone did it to him. "From now on, you'll color your hair or find another partner. I won't be seen with an old hag anymore."

She jerked him around, and before he could slug her again, she yanked on his own hair. Christ, he saw stars. It hurt that bad. Before he could get back at her, she slapped a handful of his own hair into his face. He looked at it and was shocked to see that it, too, was all silverish gray.

"You might want to take your own advice, dumbass. You have more gray than I do. Not to mention, your beard is mostly white too. How old are you now? Forty? Forty-five? You could almost pass for Santa Claus. You're even built like the jolly old fuck is." When she walked away from him, limping and holding her head, he decided to see what the fuck she was talking about. And got up to look in the bathroom mirror.

Douglas wasn't just surprised but shocked by how much gray was on his face. Even his hair, usually so dark that it looked like it was blue, was mostly gray and silver, too. Deciding, for the first time in about...well, he didn't know how long it had been, but he decided to shave off his facial hair. It was a good deal harder than he thought it would be.

It was too long for the razor that he had. He didn't trust Shelly enough to hand her the scissors to have her trim him up so he was sawing at his face with whatever he could find. Which just happened to be a pair of the smallest damned scissors that he'd ever seen. What a woman would use them for was beyond him, but he worked at it for over two hours, thinking about halfway through his chopping job that it might have been better off being all over gray.

Exhausted and his face bleeding from the hair mostly being pulled out rather than cut, he sat down on the commode and laid his head on the sink. He was also out of shape, he realized. Douglas couldn't remember the last time that he'd been on a walk that didn't have him resting after a few minutes. He'd been a runner when he'd been younger, loving the way his body responded when he had to make a quick getaway. But no more. He was fat. And gray. Looking in the mirror again, he also realized, too, that he was old. Shelly had been wrong about his age, too. He was nearly thirty-nine years old. He couldn't remember when that happened to him either.

"That would make Carrie…let me remember." He usually hated to talk to himself, but today, there wasn't anyone around that would help him so he tried to work things out. "She'd been fourteen years younger than me, so that would make her twenty-five. That doesn't seem right."

But no matter how many times he worked it out in his head, she was twenty-five, and he was almost forty. Christ, where had all the years gone. Not to mention, he thought he was much too young to be having so much in the way of a gray head. Then he remembered his father.

Dad had been nearly all white when he'd celebrated his fiftieth birthday. Also, he'd gotten quite bawld by then, too. Mother had had a lot of streaks in her hair that were colorless but he didn't know if that was because she'd had it made that way or what. Another thing that he remembered was finding the bald spot as big as his fist on the back of his mother's head when he'd walked behind her while she sat at the dining room table.

He'd been so shocked by that. Douglas hadn't said a word about it. Just the thought of her being naked in the back of her head had him picking up the mirror that was there and looking at the back of his own head.

And there it was. His mother's bad hair. Not only did he have a place back there that had not a root of hair, but it was nearly as big as his entire head, with just a few sprinkles of his hair that seemed to know to float over it. Hiding—not so well how he was aging much worse than his parents had.

He needed to do something. Anything to make it so that he didn't look older than he was. Coming out of the bathroom, he had a towel wrapped around his head like he'd only just popped out of the shower and went into the bedroom to their suite. Pulling on the first thing that he touched, a dark suit that usually reminded him of a funeral cloak, he was headed out the door when he remembered that he was dead. Or thought to be dead.

"Mother fuck." Standing there, with his fist wrapped around the handle of the door, he cursed a string of curse words, mostly things that he'd made up, for ten minutes. Then he turned, needing to find something to destroy. All he found was an empty room of even a television. The hotel hadn't replaced it since he'd knocked it off the wall when he'd first started living there. He'd not been able to leave then, either.

There was no sign of Shelly either, thinking that she might be willing to allow him to — well, willing wouldn't be what she'd call it, but he would knock her around a bit more. He loved to hurt the bitch because she'd give as good as she got until he used his anger to knock her out. Smiling, he leaned his head against the still-closed door.

There had to be something that he could do. Other than, of course, go out and tell the world that he was indeed alive and that he should be in trouble for all the shit that he'd been up to before and after his supposed death. It was completely unfair that people didn't have a sense of humor about things. He could have made his comeback, and no one would have batted an eye if they were to have a little fun about it.

~*~

Carrie was home, not her home but that of Archie. It was a fucking huge house with plenty of room for her to choose any room that she wanted. However, it was Archie who told her that the master suite had been redone and that it was ready for her to use.

"I've been working on the rooms one at a time. But since you've come along, Sunny has sent over some magical beings. I don't want to freak you out and tell you what they are, and they're finishing up the other rooms. I'm having all the rooms updated, mostly the kitchen, because it's really outdated." She asked him where he was sleeping. "I've been staying at Wrangler's house with him while his home and the others are being built. Again, with magic."

"What are they? No, don't tell me. They're unicorns. No, that wouldn't be safe for them. Faeries? Yes, it has to be one of those." He told her that it was faeries, but there were a lot of them. "Of course. I don't know that I believe you or not but I'm guessing that I'll have to get used to a lot of things before this is done."

"Yes. I have, as well. I did want to talk to you about being the leap leader with me. It's a good job to have. I can take care of the others in the leap that have been neglected for a long time." She asked him what she'd be doing if he took the job. "Mostly, finding ways to help the people that depend on us. If you see something that needs to be taken care of, you can have it taken care of. Right now I'm thinking that we need to upgrade some of the houses for the elderly. Most of the leap is older. The young people have been leaving because nothing was done to keep them around. I want to take care of that too."

"That's a great idea. I like that." The two of them talked about what needed to be done to bring in more people. After he left, telling her that he had to go and see Johisa about the accounts, she decided to take a nap. She'd been resting as much as she could. It felt nice to just be able to lie on the couch and close her eyes.

Waking up, not knowing what had startled her to wake, Carrie sat up and looked around the room. Sitting across from her, a woman was staring at her. When asking her who she was got an answer that she'd not expected. Nor believed, for that matter.

"My name is Shelly Gibson. I'm dead. Or at least I think that's what happened to me. I'm not entirely sure. Anyway, I'm...I was your brother's girlfriend up until—To be honest, I'm not doing well with times. I can hang out a little, but then I get sort of weak and sleep, I guess. Only to wake up someplace else. Like here. I've been trying to find you since I passed away." Carrie asked her how she had died. "Douglas beat me all the time. I think that it was our thing. Anyway, I read in the paper about you being a hero and we got into a fight. That doesn't matter, not really, but he beat me up again. Snatched some of my hair out of my head too. I ended up in the emergency room because I started throwing up. The doctors there told me that I had a concussion, a bad one, and that they needed to take some x-rays. I had a brain bleed, they told me when the doctor came to see me. After giving me something to calm me down...I think I died before they could operate on me. At least, that's what I'm thinking. I don't know how I died other than I just showed up at the hotel where I'd been staying, and Douglas didn't acknowledge me in any way."

"So you're telling me that you're dead and that my brother had something to do with it. I don't know what your game is, but Douglas is dead." Shelly told her that he faked his death so that he didn't get killed when some of the people that he borrowed money from would leave him alone.

"I'm sorry. This is a lot to take in. He's alive. And has been all this time. While I don't want to believe you, this does sound like something that he'd do."

As she was sitting there, talking to Shelly about some of the things that had happened since her brother faked his death, Nash joined her on the couch. He asked her who she was talking to.

"Shelly Gibson. Do you know her?" He shook his head telling her that he did not. "She claims, and I have to admit that I'm believing what she says about him, but she told me that he killed her. Indirectly, I guess, but he slapped her around, and that was how she ended up in the ED. She died before they could take care of something—"

"You don't believe me?" Carrie turned to Shelly and told her that it was a lot to take in. "I guess I can understand that. It's not every day that a dead person would visit you. How long have the dead been coming to you?"

"You're my first." She looked at Nash when he cleared his throat. "She's talking to me about how I don't believe her. I feel like Alice and that I've tumbled down a rabbit hole."

Nash threw back his head and laughed. "You're such a delight. However, if she's speaking to you from the beyond, I'd believe her. I just checked with the hospital, and a woman died two days ago from blunt force. Her body hasn't been identified, but I was able to have the faerie that I sent there to verify that it's the woman you're talking to."

"Now, what do I do?" Nash told her that Archie was on his way home, and he wanted to see if he could see her as well. "So we just hang out? I don't know about you, but I'm feeling decidedly overwhelmed right now."

"I don't blame you, love. This is something new to all of us." Carrie didn't comment on the fact that there were three more men in the room with them. All of them looked as if they'd had their throat cut out. She asked Nash to describe what the men looked like that he'd killed. "One of them is taller than the other two. He has blond hair and a tattoo on his face of a teardrop. The second man was shorter and very heavy. He had as many as three chins. His hair was dark, almost black. The third man. Let me think. By the time I got to him, he'd shot at me three times. I don't know if you can see it or not but he didn't have his right hand after I was finished with him. Is that them?"

"Yes. All three of them are here and they're demanding that I bring them back to life. I'm not going to do that. I don't know that I can but I wouldn't anyway." Nash told her that he was glad for that. Just then, Archie came into the room and sat down on her other side. "Can you see them too?"

He looked around the room until she pointed out that Shelly was sitting on the couch and that the three men were in the doorway to go outside. Shaking his head, he said that he couldn't but that he'd be there for her if they came at her.

"You think they can harm me?" He said he didn't know anyone else who could see them, so he hadn't any idea if they could or not. "Good point. Nash can't see them either. I'm assuming that this is some of the magic that I got from you. If so, why can't you see them too?" Archie took her hand into his and kissed the back of it.

"I don't have any idea. But I would say that's about right." He looked in the direction of where Shelly was sitting again. "I don't know how to help you on this other than to be with you when you're working. Do you know what it is that you're supposed to do for the dead? Have you any clue that would help them or something?"

"I suddenly have a bunch of information in my head. When you touched me, it was just there. I can help them, but not illegal. Also, I can do things for those who have been murdered. However, if anything happens, like they try to make me kill someone for them, I can send them away." She looked back at the three men that had murdered before. "I can tell what their deeds are, too. Those three men that you killed, Nash? They have a long list of people that they've murdered. I even know where the bodies are."

She thought of their mother, a woman who deserved to be sent away more than anything. Carrie had heard about how she'd treated her sons and wanted them to be safe. It occurred to her that she knew that she'd been causing trouble to the other dead people in the holding area. What she hadn't been aware that it was called.

"What the fuck are you doing?" The moment that the elderly woman spoke, she knew who it was. LouCinda Sheppard had made her way to her. It was Shelly who confirmed it for her by telling her that she'd been harming the dead since her death. "I asked you a question. What do you think you're doing with my ungrateful curs of my children?"

"Guys? Your mother is here. At least, that's who I think it is. There is an elderly man with her, but he committed suicide. I have to figure out how to speak to him." Both of them stood up, but they sat down again when she asked them to. "She's complaining about how you all are responsible for her death. I don't believe that any more than I believe that the world is going to be all up in smoke in ten minutes."

"What is she saying about us? I'm curious to know." Carrie told the two brothers how she was bitching about dying before they did. "She wanted us to be dead. Tell her who you are to me, love. I'm betting that gets her really pissed off."

"You're not supposed to be here without an appointment." LouCinda told her that it was her house and she'd do as she pleased. "But it's not your house. It's mine and Archies. We're going to be getting married soon too. Might even have a bunch of little cubs and tell the world how we made you a grannie. Won't that be awesome?"

"It will not. You get that notion out of your head right now. I'll not have you...who are you anyway? Some tart that thinks to get my son to marry you? He won't. I don't know why he's thinking that he can do a damned thing without my approval, but none of them are going to be married. Over my dead body."

"Well, that's easy enough. You are dead, dumbass. And you'll keep control of yourself, or I'll send you away. Now, as I was saying, we're going to be living here and making this house a great deal more fun than you ever allowed. And when the holidays come around, we'll put up the biggest tree we can find. In every room of the house, too." She glanced at Shelly, who told her that she was there to help her if she needed it. "Now I have a helper. Your mother is still bitching, but I'm ignoring her for now. What do you want done with her? I can send her away; that's what I'd do, or we can send her back to where she came from."

"Away." She asked Archie if he wanted to ask his brothers. Perhaps they'd want some questions answered. "I'll ask them. That's a good point. Though I will have to admit, whatever spews from her mouth would be a lie."

After Archie spoke to his brothers by the

way of the link that they all shared, they all agreed
to send her away. Her father, as well. Asking Shelly
what the repercussions would be if she did that,
Shelly said that nothing would come back on her
as that's what she's around for. Seeding LouCinda
away was fine by her so she simply told her she
was no longer welcome in this plane or the other.
That she was forbidden to come back again.

When she disappeared, the elderly man
stepped forward. There was so much anger and
evilness coming from him that the air surrounding
the man was bright red with it. While she thought
of that, she looked at Shelly. Her air was blue. And
according to the information that was in her mind,
she wasn't perfect but she wasn't evil either.

"She's gone. Now, your grandfather? What
do you want to do with him?" Archie said that he
had a question for him. After he asked the old man,
she waited for his answer like everyone else did.

"Why did I treat you so badly? Christ, you
weren't wanted in the first place. And if I'd of had
my way, I would have killed your father the first
time he had sex with my baby girl. But she didn't
mind it as much until she got knocked up. I hated
the six of you more than...well, my own mate. And

I hated her with every breath that I took for trying to make my little girl into her image. She was easy to kill, unlike the lot of you. You've no idea how many times I would try to smother you. Drowning you in the tub, too. It was like you had nine lives or something. Always hanging on out of spite to me. Then that fucking bitch, Lily, came along and made it so I couldn't touch you, and that pissed me off enough that I killed my son-in-law when I couldn't kill you kids. You hung on like your... that's funny, you hung on like your life depended on it. So I guess that's right. What do you plan on doing with me? Huh? Do you think you can just toss me away like she did your mother? It's not going to happen. I'm here for good. I have friends in places like the one where I'm staying that will kill you off so that I can have my life back. Yeah, you heard me, I'm going to be alive soon and you'll see just how bad I can treat you six. Good Christ, I can't believe I was stupid enough to kill myself off when I should have turned the gun on the lot of you." Carrie understood that there were people in the world of the dead who bragged about returning the dead to the living. But it wasn't possible.

With a snap of her fingers, something that

she'd never been able to accomplish before, the man disappeared in a puff of dark red smoke. Almost like he'd exploded where he stood, and the evilness of his life was all that was left of him. Turning to Archie, she waited for a few seconds before speaking to him.

"We need to bond. I want to be assured of being able to protect your family if someone like that comes around again. It won't be your family, I don't believe so, but there might be some people that don't care for what I'm doing with their kind." Archie asked her if she was sure. "I am. I don't think I've ever been so sure of something than I am bonding with you. I'm not sure if I love you. I'm sorry about that. I don't believe that I've ever loved anyone before. I did love my parents. But I've also come to the conclusion that they weren't all that good to me anyway. It was always about themselves. And Douglas when he needed their help financially. As in him needing bail and a good attorney. "

"How often was that? I'm assuming quite frequently, knowing what little I know about him now." Carrie said it wasn't too bad when he'd been a teenager but it got so much worse when he got older. "I'm assuming that you've never been in trouble. That's why they never noticed you. Is that about right?"

"Yes. They loved each other without thought to their children. I tried acting out, getting them to at least notice me but that wasn't happening. Then Douglas started his life of crime, and that was all they could see with him. All they wanted to see, I guess. When they died, my mother passed on first, then my dad. They said that he died of a broken heart. Mom died of lung cancer because she smoked two packs of cigarettes a day up until she got lung cancer. After that, I think it was a race for her to smoke as much as she could. Stupid of her, but then I don't know that she was ever very smart. Mom seemed to be the breadwinner most of the time." Archie asked her if her mother had the money. "Yes. Dad didn't have anything before they married. Mom had married him after her parents had died, and they had left her a great deal of money. They didn't spend it on much, not even to upgrade the house, so when they died, they left it all to me. I guess when I think about it, they had noticed me and rewarded me for not causing any trouble. Douglas wasn't mentioned in the will, and as far as I can remember, he's never asked about it. Is he really still alive?"

"Yes." Archie took her hand into his before continuing. "When Shelly's body is sorted out, he'll have to leave the hotel. I'm going to go to the police station now to identify her body as well as tell them that Douglas has been there all along. I can't believe that he's not been caught. But he will be now. If you don't mind."

"No. That'll be great. One less thing that I have to concern myself with." Carrie looked around the room at the others there and back to Archie. "I've set up some rules that they have to follow. As soon as I can find a place where they can come to me, I'll make sure that no one comes to our home again."

After a quick kiss on her mouth, he left her there with his brother. Nash was going to take her around to find a suitable building—it really didn't have to be much—that she could use to make her job work better. She also had to get with the bank and make sure that her brother couldn't get into her or Archies accounts.

Chapter 3

Archie had spoken to Carrie twice since he'd gone to the police station. The first time was when he asked her if Shelly had any tattoos or marks on her body to identify her. While he could make out her face, too much damage had been done to it for a one-hundred percent identification. The turtle tattoo on her left hip, as well as 'Douglas' written around her ankle, was the perfect help he needed to claim her body and have her sent to the funeral home after the police were finished. After he collected her things, a necklace as well as her birthstone ring, the other things were left behind for the criminal case against Douglas. In addition to the clothing, she had a gun on her that they were hoping had been used in other crimes around town. It had gone to be tested just after he did his part in claiming her body for burial.

"How long have you known that Douglas was with her sharing an apartment, Archie? I mean, I have to have something for my records on it." He told the officer the truth, or at least a part of the truth, saying that Shelly had spoken to Carrie at some point. "That'll be easy enough to find out. I don't think any of us thought that he had a full-time girlfriend. I didn't think that anyone was stupid enough to be that monster's girl. But then, when she ended up at the hospital, I think the doctors said that she'd been in there quite often before that day, in fact, several times a month. I wonder all the time why women stay with men like that. I know, too, that there are women out there that beat on me. I just don't understand it."

"I don't either. Not at all. But then, I grew up with my mom beating on my dad a great deal. He never hit us. I genuinely think that he saved our lives when we were children by taking her on. Then her father started in on us. I've only recently found out that he tried to have Mother abort us by means of throwing her down the stairs a few times, and she was all for it. He did kill Dad, he told us, because he'd had sex with her. It's small wonder that any of us grew up to be halfway normal kids." Scotty laughed and said he was sorry. It didn't bother him as much as it used to, people knowing their business. As Sunny was so fond of saying, they had made them into the great men that they were now. At least, he hoped so.

"We'll go and pick him up tomorrow, but keep an eye on him until then. He'll be starving by then without her picking—you know, I wondered all the time how someone as tiny as she was could put away as much food as she would have delivered nightly. Now, I guess we all know what she'd been doing. Sharing everything with him, including her income too. Even though she's dead, they'll try her the same as if she weren't. Poor girl. She was surely beaten to crap by him." After he left there, he set one of the faeries that had been following him around to keep an eye on Douglas. Archie didn't want anyone hurt, and if they were waiting until tomorrow to arrest him, he might be desperate enough to hurt them more when they showed up.

Archie made his way to the building, where Nash said that he was with Carrie. He was both nervous and excited to be living with her as his mate. However, he was just as terrified. It wasn't as if he hadn't had sex before. It was just that he'd never had it with a mate before. Archie wanted it to be as romantic as he could make it. He spotted the florist just as he was coming out of the post office after having his address changed.

Archie had always loved rooted plants more than cut flowers. Mostly the green type, but he also loved the fragrance that flowers gave off. His favorite smell was gardenias. The tart smell they gave off reminded him of his dad and the way he would take care of those very plants outside their home. It surprised him, too, that people thought that they only came in red when they had a variety of colors. Mom was never keen on there being flowers around the house. So, as soon as he was declared dead, Mother had all the flowers destroyed by the lawn mower that were surrounding their home. Next spring, he was going to have the entire house encircled with flowers and plants year-round in honor of his dad. He thought that once he told his brothers what he was doing, they'd more than likely do it as well. Archie was also thinking of putting in a few trees, fruit ones as well as flowering ones in the back yard as well.

After getting a beautiful bouquet of flowers for Carrie, he detoured to the next house they were seeing and sat down on the floor to wait for her and Nash. He was thinking about the house that they were living in when a child wandered into the building and seemed to be making himself at home. It wasn't until he pulled a puppy out of his jacket that he thought that he knew what was going on. And who the boy was.

"Mikey? Is that you?" He looked so terrified that Archie put up both hands so that he'd see he was his friend. "It's all right. It's me, Archie Sheppard. What do you have there?"

"A dog. Mom won't let me have one at home on account of them eating everything in sight. But I thought that I could save him bits of my lunch and stuff to bring him. He's a pretty dog, and I thought that I could teach him to warn us about my daddy coming around." Mikey slapped his hand over his mouth and stared at him wide-eyed for a moment. "I was only kidding, Mr. Sheppard. I really do...I mean, my daddy don't hurt us much. I was just joking around."

"Sure you were, kid. I understand more

than anyone how parents can be mean to us. It's all right. I won't tell a soul what you said to me." He scratched the dog behind the ears and was rewarded with a lick to his hands. The dog was so wiggly that he was sure that Mikey was going to drop the little pup. But he held him tightly like he was used to having the dog be happy like that. "Where is your daddy now? Jail again?"

"No, he's out. I'm going to tell you right, Mister. He's making things hard for my mom and sister. I can sneak out before he gets too drunk sometimes but I can run on account of me putting me a pair of shoes I can grab and go." Mikey, about ten years old, looked up at him. He had a shiner that looked fresh. He asked him about it. "You're the only one that knows about my daddy, I think. Nobody does anything about him, so I'm thinking they don't see it or hear him when he's home. Last night he beat up my momma and sister so bad that Sissy had to go get some stitches. Momma told me to stay away until he left. I don't mind doing that for me, but I worry about them. He sure does hate my sister for her being a girl and all. It's not her fault she was born that way. I think that he's mean for blaming something like that on her. Don't you?"

"I don't understand that at all either. However, I know what you're saying about leaving your family to fend for themselves. You don't want to be hurt anymore, and you hate that you have to leave your family in order for you not to be. I'm sorry he's like that. I think he and my mother could have used a few lessons on hitting people that are smaller than themselves." Mikey agreed. "All right, buddy. How about I keep your pup at my house. He doesn't seem to have much trouble with what I am."

"On account of me being a bear, too. I thought he'd run when he smelled me, but he didn't do nothing but come right to me. Maybe his smeller is broken." Mikey grinned at him, knowing that he'd said it wrong. "I like you, Mr. Sheppard. You're all right. Momma said that you guys are better off without your momma. She told me that if there was a family that needed a break more than you guys did, she didn't want to meet them. I don't know what she meant by that but I think she meant it in a good way."

"Thank you. And I'm sure that she did." He held onto the pup and tried to look it over at the same time. It was the wiggliest dog he'd ever been around. Once he touched the little guy's left back paw, he whimpered but didn't bite him. "I think we should run him by the vet. Just to make sure that he's healthy. I'd really hate to take him home and find out that he was sick. My new wife would murder me."

He told Nash and Carrie where he was headed, and Carrie decided to come along. She said that if a puppy was going to be living with them, then she should get to know it. However, as soon as she got to the office, her smile dropped, and he had a feeling that there was someone else there that only she could see.

It bothered him a little that he couldn't help her when someone showed up. But then, he didn't know what he'd do if a dead man was around either. Smiling to himself, he decided that he could be as helpful as she needed by being there for her. Sometimes, he thought, it was easier just to be ready for something that happens rather than create trouble because you've been left out, like Mikey, that made better sense in his head.

"He's got an infected toenail that can be easily fixed. You said that you found this little guy?" Mikey told Brandon that he'd found him while walking back from the barn. "If I were you, I'd check out the barn more. I'm thinking that there might be a couple more dogs out there, too. I've heard tell that Mrs. Adaline's pregnant dog has gone missing. I don't know if anything happened to her cherished pet, but it's not like it to not come home. If you find her, let me know, and I'll make sure that she's all right. Even if she's not, someone needs to take care of the pups. I might have to keep him here for a couple of days. You can come by and visit him anytime you want. I'd welcome the company."

"I'll head out there now. I should mention that he wasn't fearful of either of us. Mikey is a bear, and I'm a jag, but he didn't run off when he smelled us." Brandon said the dog had a slight cold, too, and that was why, perhaps. "If we continue to take care of the little thing, will he stay with us even after the cold is gone?"

"I see no reason that would make it so that he'd not want to be in a nice house with people around. Just be nice to him and the others if you bring them home and they'll stick around. However, let me know if you decide not to keep them all. Being kind to animals is all they need to be your best friend. Not to mention a couple of good snacks, too." Brandon looked at Mikey, and he looked so serious. "It's a big responsibility for someone to take care of a puppy for you, Mikey. That'll mean that you are smart enough to know that you can't keep the little guy from being hurt by your father. If he does hurt any of them, you bring them here, and I'll call the police. Cruelty to animals isn't going to be something that I'll tolerate. Understand? And the invitation still stands about you coming to visit them all the time."

"Yes, sir. I will do that." He petted the puppy, and Archie noticed that he was more than a little upset. "Dad tried to kill him off yesterday by giving him rat poison. I knew he was going to try something, but I was able to save him. I might not be able to the next time. I'm glad that Mr. and Mrs. Sheppard are going to be able to keep him safe for me." He looked at him. "I'll work too, Mr. Sheppard so you don't have to be out a bunch of money for food. Momma said that dogs are expensive, so I'll make sure I work for him."

Archie started to tell him that he could afford the dog, but it was Carrie who spoke to the little guy. Telling him that he had to come by when he'd not get into trouble but to always come by and get some food for himself and his momma.

"I don't want to have you getting sick while paying for his food, young man. So you come by the house when it's safe for you to do so, and we'll fill you up. Then you can take some things home to your momma and sister too so they don't get sick. All right?" Archie thought Mikey had a loose screw in his neck for as hard as he was nodding. "Also, if your daddy hurts you again, you come to me. I'll take care that he understands that you work for us."

Mikey looked up at him. "If I was my daddy, I'd be more afraid of Ms. Carrie than I would be of you, Mr. Archie. She seems all nice and everything, but I know she can whop him hard enough that he'd remember his manners around her. Then, you'd take over when she was finished up with him. If'n there is anything left of him."

Even after Mikey left, he still laughed about what he'd said. Yes, Carrie was very protective of the little boy but so was he. Again, he didn't understand why people would knock around their children. It wasn't fair, nor was it very nice.

~*~

Carrie asked to use the bathroom and went there to talk to the ghost that was hanging around the vet. She was an elderly woman, she'd bet in her mid to late eighties, and there didn't seem to be any trauma surrounding her. But she did realize that maybe poison wouldn't leave any kind of markings, so she waited to be told what she wanted and how she could help.

"That's my great-grandson out there. Brandon Lipscomb. He's a bad man." Carrie asked her what she meant and then sat down on the closed commode. "I've been trying to make it hard for him to be alone with little kids, but he's a nasty man and gets away with it by telling them that he'll let their pets die if they don't let him do what he wants with them."

"You have to tell me what it is that he does. I'm sorry, Ms. Lipscomb but I need more than him just being a bad man. I think that Mikey's dad is bad, but he beats the little boy and—"

"He makes them touch him in his private parts. His dick, I guess you young people would call it. Sometimes, he'll offer them a drink of soda or something that has medicine in it. They fall asleep, and he strips them down to take pictures of them while they're naked." That was more than Carrie had thought. On the outside, he looked like a nice guy. "He's a bad man who got those ideas from his daddy when he was the vet here. No one ever thinks that…you have to stop him. He's going to hurt that little boy out there on account'a him getting away from him a lot. I don't think that young Mikey knows what he's about either."

"No, I don't think that he does. Or he wouldn't have wanted to come here no matter what. Do you know of any other kids that he's done this to?" Instead of answering her, she pointed to the ceiling. It was a tile-like ceiling, and she was told which one to pull down. "I'm going to have to get the police to do that. He could say that I did it if I just suddenly know about it. What's up there? Or do I want to know?"

"Pictures." That's all she needed to hear before she told Ms. Lipscomb that she'd take care of him. "I'm gonna wait and make sure you don't fob me off, young lady. You're new at this, and I know that. But this is as serious as the heart attack that killed me."

Reaching out to all the brothers and Archie,

she told them what she'd found out. Sunny was at the police station, finding out what kind of permits she'd need to have a big hometown picnic before the weather got too bad. She said she'd take care to make sure that the station knew about it.

"*Carrie, you're going to have to come clean about what you can see and hear. They're going to get suspicious about all the information that you have just out of the blue. I think you should just talk to one officer, I'd recommend you talk to Larry Knocks. He's a good guy with an open mind.*" She said that she'd have to talk to Archie first. "*That's a splendid idea. Yes, talk to him. In the meantime, I'm going to talk to Larry and see what he can do about it.*"

When she left the bathroom, she noticed that Brandon was talking to Mikey about how he'd have to come by once a day to do chores so that he'd be able to pay off his debt for taking care of the pup. She was so happy when Archie said he'd pay the bill. If she'd not been looking right at Brandon when the flash of anger was on his face, she would have missed it. She had a feeling that Archie had seen it as well.

"How much does the bill come to?" Brandon said that he thought that since it was Mikey's pup, he should be made to take care of the bills. "No. He's saved the little guy and I think that is payment enough. Just tell me how much it is, and I'll pay it now."

Brandon tried several times to make it so that Mikey had to work it off, but in the end, Archie put a hundred dollars on the table, and he and the little boy left the office. She hung out, waiting for the police to show up. Carrie was glad that Mikey wouldn't see whatever was in the paneling in the bathroom.

When the police showed up, they slapped a warrant into Brandon's chest and started tearing the office apart. She didn't know what they were about but when they started to poke at the panels in the office they were in, she watched as tapes fell from the ceiling and onto the floor. Brandon was put into cuffs when he tried to say that they weren't his. It surprised her so much that the man didn't figure out that he was going to prison. He kept saying that he'd not known there was anything up there, and then the police started to take down all the ceiling panels one by one, documenting what they found by recording it with one of the officers holding a camera on all the things that were being put into evidence bags. Christ, she thought, it was going to take forever to sort through all the things that they were finding. There had to be several hundred tapes and other items, and they'd not even gotten to the bathroom yet. Ms. Lipscomb asked to speak to her, and she made her way outside, and the woman followed her.

"You've made it so that I can move on now. I can't thank you enough for doing this. I'm thrilled that he's going to be in prison. If he makes it that far. I'm thinking that once he's put into jail he'll be joining me in the afterlife. I want that to happen, too. The bastard deserves whatever he gets." She agreed with her and smiled. "You're a beautiful young lady. Inside and out. I know that you'll do good things for us. I'm going to make sure I tell everyone that I know — perhaps I won't tell everyone. I'll just tell the ones that need your help that are hurting because of something that happened to them."

"Thank you for that. I do hope that you have a good afterlife from now on. You should be proud of what you've done for a lot of children. It's going to come out, and there will be no place that he's not safe from. I hope he gets everything that he deserves." She said that she knew that he would. "Don't do anything that will get you into trouble. I would hate to have to send you away."

"Oh, I won't have to. I know of a few of the children that he hurt on my side. They're just waiting for him to get to them so that they can make sure that—it's in the rules. They can harm him if he did them in real life. I made sure before I let them know that I was working with someone on the other side." Carrie told her that she had just learned all the rules. "Yes, I would imagine that you'd have to have them all memorized. Good for you. And I can't thank you enough for what you've done for us. I'm going to go on now."

She simply faded away. It was a wonderful way to watch someone pass into the next part of their journey. Feeling good about helping someone, she made her way home to get ready for Archie. He'd told her that he was with the police and that he'd be home at dinner. Thinking about that, she decided that she'd figure out what his favorite meal was and have it made for them. Carrie knew that she couldn't cook what he wanted, so she did what she could to make him feel loved. Because she did love the man very much.

"*His favorite meal is pork chops simmered in gravy with mashed potatoes. Bread too. For sopping up the leftovers. Candied carrots as well.*" Carrie asked Beau if it was his brother's or his favorite meal. "*His. Mine is spaghetti and meatballs. Lots of meatballs. Garlic bread, too. Yum. Now I want that. But he had the chops once at a diner that we found when we'd gone to Columbus once. Every time we go there, he gets the same thing. Also, cherry pie warmed up with ice cream.*"

"*That sounds really good, too.*" Beau asked her if she was cooking that. If so, he was coming over for dessert. "*No, thank you. I'm going to be his cherry pie with ice cream.*"

She thought that she might have said too much but when he laughed, telling her how much he loved her, Carrie smiled. It was nice having brothers around all the time, and she thought that she could get used to teasing them, too. She thought that they had turned out well, considering what they'd had to grow up with. Carrie was glad that their mother wasn't going to be causing any more trouble and that the grandfather was gone as well.

Realizing that it was later than she'd thought,

Carrie made sure that things were ready for dinner before going to their room to make sure that it was all ready for a night of debauchery and fun. Everything was just how she wanted it, including the fruit that she had brought to the room and the bottle of champagne. Smiling to herself about what she was going to do to him, Carrie made her way downstairs and was just heading for the kitchen again when Archie came home.

He looked beat. Hugging him and telling him that dinner was ready, he looked too exhausted to make his way to the food. Telling him what they were having perked him up a bit but when he sat down, Carrie knew that he was going to be falling asleep in his food if she didn't do something.

She had no idea how to be sexy and especially didn't want to make a fool of herself in front of him. Putting her feet into his lap, she wiggled her toes over his hardening cock until he looked at her. Smiling, she asked him if he was all right.

"You keep that up, and the food will be wasted. I'm exhausted but not that tired." She thought about what she'd said to Beau about being his dessert.

"If you clean your plate, I'll spread fruit all

over my body for you to nibble on then do the same for you. I already have the next part of dinner all ready for you." He asked her what she meant. "I have cherries that I'm going to put on my nipples. Some pretty strawberries on my pussy, then I'm going to—what are you doing now?"

"I'm taking you to bed. I'm suddenly starved for you and not food." He dragged her across the dining room and to the stairs. When she nearly tripped, he put his shoulder into her stomach and carried her up the stairs on his shoulder. Once they were in their room, he locked the door and turned to her. Christ, she didn't think that he could get any more sexy than he was right then. And she loved him with all her heart. "You've no idea how long I've been thinking about you naked. Daily. No, hourly. I've wanted to take you to any hard surface and take you until we're both sated that I can't think beyond that most of the time."

"I love you so much, Archie. Please, make me yours." He kissed her, and Carrie could taste him deliciously when he swept his tongue along her lips and then into her mouth. It was the most wonderful thing, having a man that you loved to make love to your entire self.

Chapter 4

Archie slowly undressed Carrie, careful of touching her lightly as he did so. His fingers burned against her skin. Her mouth, when he touched his fingers to her lips, was moist and swollen from his kisses. There was nothing that he loved more than this woman and now he was going to get to show her just how much he did. At her slow sigh, he leaned back from her body ever so slightly and smiled at her.

"Your touch, it's like I'm being set on fire on my breasts and pussy. I'm so wet, Archie, that I can feel it sliding down my thighs." His smile widened, thinking of the very part of her that he wanted more than anything. "If you don't make me come soon, it's going to be a longer wait for you. Let me come, and I'll be able to come with you when you're inside of me. I ache with need now."

He had her blouse off. It had occurred to him that she'd not put on any kind of gown to sleep in nor anything to tempt him once they were in bed together. It was pointless to him for her to have something sexy on for him. Archie thought that she was sexy anyway she was dressed or, as it turned out, how she was undressed.

Fingers tangled in his hair, and all he could think about was being inside of her. As she rode him still dressed, her hips moving back and forth in quick hard strokes, he cupped her ass and bought her to him so that she was riding his covered cock. When he bit down on her nipple, tasting her blood as it filled his mouth, she cried out her release, and he growled at her to come again.

Kissing her mouth and then nuzzling her neck, Archie thumbed her nipples until they swelled. They were hard and thick, and he wanted to have them bare in his mouth again. But the need to mark her, make her his, was making his cat scream at him. He loved his mate, too, and needed to know that no one else would touch her. As soon as she came again, screaming out his name, Archie let his cat, using his teeth and mouth to take his part of her. Archie felt the savage in him bite her deeply. Her second scream nearly had him coming in his pants.

He held her to him. Archie felt his heart still pounding in his chest, and he'd had to work hard at calming his cat, but right now, both of them were satisfied that they had marked her. When she lifted her head, he could see that he'd missed a few drops of her blood and leaned to lick them off her. Her moan had him sucking hard on her flesh until she started to ride him again.

"If we stay here much longer, I'm going to lay you out on this floor and drink from your pussy. I can smell you. You're aroused, wet, and hot." She stopped moving, and he put his hands on her hips to give him just a little more of her. "Do you have any idea how much I want you?"

"I can feel your cock. So I'd say, yes, I can tell." He stared at her for several seconds, then laughed. "This isn't funny. And if you think this is going to distract me from what you said to me, you're fucking nuts."

"I am at that. And no, I don't think it's going

to distract you." He kissed her again, taking his time moving his tongue over the darkest and tastiest part of her mouth, absorbing her into his as he rocked up into her heat with her lower half still dressed. "Never would I use sex to make you forget what's going on around us. No matter how tempting you are. And you are so tempting."

Making his way down her throat to her breasts, he suckled hard on the large tip and moaned when she held his head tightly to her. Moving her around, putting his hands into the back of her jeans, Archie let a little of his cat go so that he could use his sharp nails to rip her pants and panties off her. The sound was much more sexier than he thought it would be. It also made him want to tear all her clothing off her from now on.

Lying her on the bed, he took his time to undress himself. With his shirt already off, he unbuckled his belt and then slowly removed it from his pants, coming out of the loops to hold it one at a time, never taking his eyes off of his one true love. As soon as it was free, Archie dropped it to the floor, loving again the sound of the buckle hitting the floor. Then he unsnapped his jeans.

"I've never watched a man undress before." Sitting up on her hands behind her, Carrie licked her lips, causing him pain when she did so, and watched him unsnap his pants one snap at a time. Watching her watch him, he saw her eyes darken in desire. Her tongue moistened her lips while he felt his air catch in his lungs. When she took her foot and rubbed it up and down his cock that was leaking cream all over his boxers, Archie grabbed her foot and held tightly against him while she worked him over. "That's an amazing feeling, Archie. You're so hard and hot. It's like I've laid my foot on an open flame. And your cream between my toes is like nothing I've ever experienced before."

He couldn't speak. He was having enough difficulty just breathing. When she moved her other foot to his cock, Archie released her and leaned over her while she played with his cock. He needed to hold on to the bed before he passed out. If he came right now, he knew that he'd be out of it for days. Standing up, removing her feet, Archie tore his own pants off and grinned at her when she cried out as another quick climax took her.

Turning her in the bed so that her legs hung

over the side, he seated himself between her legs and spread her nether lips wide. Watching as her cream slowly made its way to the bed, he leaned in and licked her from gate to clit, stopping long enough to suckle of her until she cried out. Pulling her closer to his mouth, he devoured her over and over while sliding his fingers into her. Christ, he thought, this was the most fun he'd had during sex in his life.

When she closed her thighs around his head, he looked up at her. She'd been crying, and he was sorry for that. Asking her if she was all right, she snapped at him that she needed to come. Having no idea why he thought that was so funny, Archie leaned into her for one more kiss and stood up. His cock was wet, too, the tip of it nearly black, it was so full and painful.

"Take me. Or not, but I'm going to come." He leaned over her, taking her mouth with his own as he put his knee between her thighs. "Please? Please give me what I need."

He didn't hesitate, but when he felt her heat and wetness, he slammed forward, taking her throat into his mouth and suckling hard. When her skin broke, tasting her blood again, he held her bottom close to him, tiling it upward so that he could go deeper. He fucked Carrie with everything that he had left, watching her face again.

When he felt his own climax race to his balls, feeling like they were ready to explode at any moment, he held her tightly while he slowed to have her catch up to him. However, he didn't think that she liked that when she dug her heels into his lower back and held his ears. Her words, 'fuck me,' were slurred, and he couldn't help but do what she wished and fucked her through four quick releases before he let himself go.

Archie threw back his head when he felt his cock release. He'd come before, even today, but this was nothing like he'd ever experienced before. It was as if he was being turned inside out, then righted again over and over. Then when he was ready to drop atop her, his body finally emptied, Archie felt something akin to having a sword being stuck into the bottom of his cock and through it to the end. It was that painful. Crying out, he held Carrie to him so that neither of them moved.

Putting her hands on his cheek, he looked at her. Everything was blurry, and he was still in slight pain. But when her body, her sheath, rolled around his cock, he released again and felt everything blackout for him.

When he woke, only seconds, he thought, he was on his back, and Carrie was in his arms. Thinking about what had happened, wondering what had hurt him so much, Archie started to feel something roll over him. It started in his head, and gently, it seemed to him move down over his body until he was—with Carrie still holding him—doing things to not just his body, but he thought that it was moving into his heart, lungs, and blood. Closing his eyes against the sudden bright lights, he heard Carrie cry out then nothing.

Waking up, the two of them were in bed. Someone had moved them to the center of the bed and covered them up. Wondering who might have done something like that, he wasn't the least bit upset when he thought that they'd not just seen him naked but Carrie as well. She rolled over, laying her head on his chest as he ran his fingers up and down her back.

"I don't know about you, but I think that I'd rather not have that kind of sex again. I'm still reeling from it. And I feel...I don't know, I feel everything. I can hear, too, better than I did before." She looked up at him, resting her head on her fist. "You look different too. Like, you were a big man before, but I think you're bigger. I know that your hair is lighter, too, longer."

"I think that since we bonded, we got the magic that comes with it. I don't know. But we do have to talk about a couple of things." She asked him if it was about the ghosts. "That wasn't it, but now that you mention it. Are there any in this room? I can't see them if there is."

"No. They're forbidden to come into this house unless it's an emergency. The building that I'm going to use is ready and waiting for them to use. Also, there will be hours set in stone for when they can come to me as well." He thought that was a wonderful idea and told her so. "Shelly, she's helping me, told me that unless I wanted them to be bothering me all the time, I needed to start some rules from the start."

"Good. I like that. We'll test that later. We have to talk about the leap. Things are going on that need someone's attention and —" She told him that she would help him with it. And that he should take it without having Josiha around. "I was thinking that too. He wouldn't have much in the way of information for me with how he'd been running things. I might run into one or two issues later, but for now, like you, I'm going to set up ground rules."

The two of them talked about the leap for a while then Carrie decided that she needed to get up. For the two of them, it was much harder than he thought that it should have been. Standing in front of the mirror, holding onto the vanity, he had to laugh at himself at how bad he looked. But he did notice that she was right in saying that his hair was longer. He wondered if it was because they were bonded or something else. He wasn't going to worry about it just yet. They were headed to the leap house when he remembered that Nash was supposed to be going with them.

"Can you come to the house? I need to take over the leap." Nash asked if Carrie was going, and when he told him yes, he said that Sunny would come as well. *"Good idea. Also, we've decided that we're not going to have Josiha stick around for us. I think with the way things were left by him, we'd be better off learning as we go."*

"Excellent idea. Yes, that's good. Do you expect to be down with the magic?" Archie said that he

didn't really know what to expect. *"All right. We'll play this by ear. We're about to your house now, and we'll walk to the leap house."*

He was glad that he remembered to take his brother. Even more so that Sunny was going to help out with keeping an eye on Carrie. He wasn't worried that something would happen, he didn't want to be left alone if the magic did take him down. Smiling, he was thrilled beyond words that he and Carrie were going to be doing this. He thought that it was going to be good for everyone concerned.

~*~

Carrie hated the leap house. The few times that she'd been there, it had been horrid and smelly. It wasn't just because it smelled like a wet dog; she had no idea why that was what she thought, but it also looked like it hadn't been cleaned in centuries. She thought for sure that it hadn't, not by the way things looked right now. She hinted around, asking if the meeting between them could be done outside instead of in the sweltering heat of the building. Everyone, thankfully, agreed. Carrie let Archie do the talking.

"Josiha, we, Carrie and I, have decided to

take the job of leap leader." The man nodded, but
Carrie noticed that his wife, Alma, was shaking
her head. "I'm sorry. Is there a problem now?
Something that we need to talk about?"

"He didn't say to me that he was leaving.
I've decided that we're not." It was Sunny who
told them that they both had to agree, but in the
end, it was Josiha's decision. "Well, I've decided
that I'm not going to give up the magic. I know
what is going to happen to the two of us when you
take over, and I'm not going to give up my life
after all this time. I have things that I wish to do."

"I've been trying to talk to her, Archie but
she's a stubborn old goat and won't let me get
out of this job." Before Archie could say anything,
Alma told Josiha to shut his mouth that she was
the one in charge. "She thinks that she is. She's no
more in charge than I want to stay here. I'm tired,
Archie. I don't have it in me to do this—"

"Shut up, you old fool. You just don't seem
to get it that I'm not going to give up this life. We
have magic, money, and a house. Not as nice as
theirs but we have one that we can have a roof
over our head. I don't want to die. Do you hear
me? I do not want to end my life now that we don't

have to work anymore." Carrie started to point out that they'd have to be the leap leaders, but Alma cut her off, too. "No. We'll just keep doing what we've been doing all along. No one gives a crap if we show up to meetings or not. Hell, no one cares if we even have a meeting anymore. Dying wasn't part of the plan that I had when we were asked to do this. I just wanted the magic and the immortality. Working was never anything that I wanted to get involved in."

"Then what you're saying is that you only took the job because you were too lazy to do anything else. Is that what you're saying?" Alma admitted that was exactly what she was saying, and it was stupid of her to think that at this late in the game, she wanted to change things around. Sunny snorted before continuing. "Well, that's tough shit. Archie is set to take the job. If Josiha wants to keep his job, I suggest that the two of them fight it out. That's what is to happen next. Archie is several hundred years younger and if it comes to that, his brother Nash can take over the fight if it gets to be too much for him. I don't personally see that happening, but you never know. After that, if the two of them are drained, again, I don't see that, then the next in line is me."

Sunny simply shifted into a large dragon, spitting out flames as she reached a great height and bulk before shifting back to herself and smiling at the couple.

Josiha laughed. It was something that she'd never heard him do since she'd been around, so she thought it was odd. But the harder he laughed, pointing out to his wife that they had her there, it was Alma who laughed this time.

"You don't get it, do you? Josiha, you never were the brightest bulb in the basket, were you? They're talking about killing you off, you old fool. Not me. I'm not in charge. I just put up with you so that I could live forever. Not only that, but the pay was great, too. Even the money that was in the account for the leap...Christ, you never noticed a damned thing. I've been stealing from there for centuries, and you never had one single clue."

That seemed to be just what Sunny had been waiting for, and she put up her hand, and Alma disappeared. Just poof, she wasn't in the yard with them any longer. Everyone just stared at her as she stood there smiling. Then, it occurred to her when Josiha disappeared as well.

"You knew this. You knew that she was stealing the funds meant for the leap." Sunny shook her head and pointed to Archie. Carrie turned and looked at him. "Why didn't you tell me what was going to happen here today? I would have helped. I don't know how, but I would have."

"We've been considered leap leaders since we bonded the other day." Her face heated up when she realized what he was talking about. "Josiha came to me that day and asked me if he could speak to me. As you know or might not know, Alma has been following us around to make sure, I'm guessing, that he didn't just hand it over to me. Josiha told me everything. Not only had Alma been stealing from the leap, but she'd been running some of the leap off for various reasons because she knew that if the counting of the leap dropped to a certain number, then the king of all the leaps would give more money to this one to make changes. To make changes to the land or improve homes, whatever was needed to bring it back to a solid number."

"And she counted on this. At some point, she was making sure that she went with a large sum of money. Why would she think that they were going to die?" Archie told her what the rules stated. "I didn't know that it was their decision to stay or not. I'm guessing by the way things went that Josiha had made the decision for the two of them. That she was going to end her life no matter what."

"No. I decided that when I spoke to my mom." She asked Sunny what she meant. "Alma had been complaining about the leap running out of money for a while now, so I had someone checking into it. It wasn't until just then that we knew it was her. Stupidly on her part, she fully admitted to her being the one who was stealing from the leap and how long she'd been doing it. I didn't kill her, mores the pity. Alma was taken to our leap prison. She'll live out her days, centuries, and centuries there as a prisoner for her part in the theft. Alma will be required to work off the debt that she incurred until it's paid in full. Then, after a time, she'll die. Fade, whatever is needed to get her out of the system. Thank you for helping with it." She told her that she'd not done anything. "Oh, but you did. When you showed up here at Archie's side, it made it so much easier to get her to confess. She had to brag to someone, and why not a fellow woman."

"What about you? I mean, you're a woman too the last time I checked." Her face heated up. "Not that I go around checking on you being a woman. It was just...I got it mixed up in my head. I didn't...perhaps you can change the subject now."

"I will." Sunny laughed. "You know, I really love you, Carrie. You're kind and funny. I don't think there is a better person for the job than you and Archie. Even my mom thinks that you two will do great things now that you're in charge."

"I hope so. I want to make this a safe and wonderful place for other leap members to have a family and be able to grow with us." Sunny hugged her, and the four of them headed home. The leap house was going to be gone though, then torn down. According to the men who were going to take care of it, the building was too old to save, and the foundation was much too broken to be able to salvage. Carrie was glad. The place would forever smell like it does now, she thought.

Nash and Archie were walking behind her and Sunny when they got to their driveway. As soon as she stepped onto the porch, she felt that something was off. Hearing the small whimper of someone, she turned to see a little girl who had been beaten badly hiding in the corner of the porch under the swing. Going to her, she cried out as soon as she touched her. She called to Archie to hurry.

"She's Mikey's sister." The little girl told them that Mikey had gone back to get their mom, that she'd been beaten up by their dad, and that he had an axe. Leaping over the railing, Archie never touched the ground as a man but shifted into his beast as he took off toward what she could only assume was Mikey's home. Nash, shifting too, followed, leaving her and Sunny there to be with the little girl. Archie spoke to her as she was getting the little girl into the house.

"Bring the car when you can. I don't know what we'll find, but I'm sure that I can't go around like this. I'm sorry I left you to deal with this." She said that she would when she got the little girl settled. *"Her name is Sissy. I've spoken to Mikey a few times about his dad. I love you, baby. Please be careful when – "* When he didn't finish, she paused in wiping Sissy's face to find that she'd been cut badly by someone. *"Honey, call the police for us. Their mother is gone."*

"I'm coming. Sissy is going to need stitches, and

we'll have to take them to the hospital anyway." She was crying when she saw how badly Sissy was beaten. The child had fresh and old wounds on her small body that made her want to find her father and kill him herself. As soon as she got Sissy in the car, Sunny got in the front seat with her, and the two of them didn't speak on the way to where Archie and Nash were. She told her through their link what was going on. She asked her if she could drive.

"Yes. I wish that I could shift. I'd take care of the bastard myself." Sunny touched her fingers to her forehead, and they drove a bit slowly to the house. Neither of them said a word as they made their way around the police cars and the two ambulances that were there. Her heart hurt for what they came upon.

The mother was lying in the yard with an axe in her head. It was a horrific sight, one that she knew would be burned into her memory for a very long time, if not forever. She didn't call out to Archie, knowing that if he was busy, she might distract him enough that he'd be hurt. Carrie hoped that he was killing the father slowly for what he'd done. The man deserved whatever he got and then some.

Sissy was put into one of the ambulances, and Carrie went with her to the hospital. Holding her hand, she wondered what was going to happen to the two children now that their parents, both of them, she hoped, were gone. She was going to talk to Archie to see what the sloth would do with them. If anything, she'd adopt them into their family so that they'd never have to worry about their life again.

The sloth leader joined them at the hospital. Sissy had been sedated so they could check her body for other injuries. She told the older man, Roger, what she knew about what had happened at the house. She also told him that their mother was gone and that she'd been killed by her husband.

"He's not her husband. Her mate, either. The children, both of them are from her true mate. I don't know that Albert killed her mate, but he moved into her home not long after he was buried. I didn't know about it. We were having a bit of a crisis that had taken me away from the sloth for a couple of months. When I returned a few days ago, I was informed about what was going on. As a matter of fact, it was my intention to take her under my protection so that she'd be safe. I'm sorry to realize that I waited too long to do anything." She asked him about the children. "That would be up to their biological grandmother. I'm not sure that she'd take them in, but they'll be protected forever by the sloth."

They were going to keep Sissy for a few days. She was extremely dehydrated as well as very undernourished. She finally had to know what had happened to Mikey and reached out to Archie. His anger was apparent, and when she asked him if he was all right, he told her that he wasn't. He also didn't think he'd ever be again.

"He's dead. Margo was able to get in a few slices to his face and throat before he tossed the axe at her. I'm not sure of all the details yet, but he bled out in the woods behind her home. I wished that I could have taken care of him myself, but I believe this is better. What have you heard from Roger concerning the children? By the way, Mikey is beaten up badly but will survive. He's going to be in the hospital for a few days longer. I'm to understand that Sissy is staying there too." She told him what Roger had told her. "Good. If she doesn't take them in, would you mind if we did? I know it's a lot to ask, but—"

"I was thinking the same thing. Even if she does take them in, I'd like to be a part of their lives from now on. They need someone around that can show them that their lives were not the norm."

Chapter 5

Douglas hadn't said a word since he'd been arrested while coming out of the motel four days ago. He wanted to find and ask Shelly what the fuck she'd done, but no one was telling him anything. She was going to pay for this shit if she had told where he was. This time, he might well kill her. Things were not going as planned, and he was pissed off.

Yesterday, he'd demanded to speak to his sister. He knew as soon as he was told they'd contact her to see if she wanted to talk to him that it was her and not Shelly who had figured out where he'd been. He wasn't sure how she'd done it, but it would be just like her to go snooping around in shit that wasn't any of her concern.

"You've been asking about Shelly Gibson.

Well, I'm finally able to tell you that she died a week and a half ago from a brain bleed brought on by blunt-force trauma. She was coherent enough when she showed up at the emergency department to tell everyone that the two of you had had a fight and that it was you who had hit her several times about the head and face. You're going to be charged with her murder. There are other charges too that are pending so I'd not expect to be getting out all that soon." He could only stare at the woman officer when she then asked him what he wanted for dinner. "The menu that you got at lunch needs to be turned in now. If you don't tell me what you want, then I'm—"

"What the fuck do you mean, Shelly's dead? That's not possible." Breaking his code of silence seemed not so important when he'd learned of her supposed death. "I just saw her a few days ago. There is no way that she's been gone that long. What the fuck are you playing at?"

"Playing at? Nothing. She went into a coma on the operating table and never recovered. As I said to you, she had a brain bleed that was well advanced when they opened her up to work on her." Douglas said that she was a liar. "Whatever.

I don't care if you believe me or not. Are you going to tell me what you wish for dinner or not?"

"I demand that you bring her here this minute." She said that once he gave her his order, then she'd do just that. He looked over the menu, thinking that this was one of the worse jokes anyone had ever played on him. After ordering, the officer walked away. Douglas waited ten minutes before he started yelling about Shelly. Finally, the door at the other end opened up, and he could see her in the overhead mirror that she had a brass colored jar in her hand. "What's that?"

"Shelly Gibson. There wasn't anyone to claim her body, so Mr. Sheppard did it. Since she had no family to speak of, he had her cremated. Also, I brought you the newspaper so that you can read about it yourself." He snatched the newspaper out of her hand and leaned back to read the front-page article. "You can have that copy. There are several more of them around, too."

"It says here that she was murdered. You're not pinning that on me. I had nothing to do with her bleeding out." If the woman said anything, he was no longer paying attention. Reading about his long-time lover's demise was upsetting him enough.

Douglas read it four times before he let it sink in that she might well be as dead as he'd been told. Looking at the vase that the cop had brought with her, he could see the nameplate on the bottom of the jar with not just her name but the dates of both her birthdate as well as her death. He couldn't believe that no one thought that he'd be interested in knowing that she'd died. He'd wasted a great deal of his time in yelling about her when he could have been trying to get someone else to come and — It occurred to him that she'd told the emergency department that he'd killed her, and that was why he was stuck behind bars. He needed an attorney. Now.

His meal was brought to him at six. Having enough food to fill him up was wonderful after spending so much time locked in the hotel room without any means of getting something to fill the void in his belly. The fact that the article said that he'd been the one that she'd claimed had killed her, he surmised that they'd known he was stuck in the hotel room and hadn't come to see him. No one had brought him any food or water either. Fuckers.

Finishing up his meal, he laid on his cot and thought about what he was going to do now that he was stuck in jail. There was no way that they could pin the death of Shelly on him. It would mean that they were taking her word over his own. And who was alive to do that? Only him. So that was taken care of.

"Now what?" What else did they have him for? Nothing that he could think of right off the top of his head. He'd not even resisted arrest when they picked him up. Douglas hadn't had any insurance to claim, so that couldn't have been it. So he'd faked his death? So what? It's not like he hurt anyone by him doing that. Of course, he did plot to have his sister robbed several times, but again, who were they going to believe over him? His sister? Not likely. Even the men that he'd had working for him weren't around anymore. It did stick in his crawl that they'd told him about Shelly. Damn, but he was going to miss that bitch. Sitting up on the side of his cot, he looked at the mirror again to find out what the clicking noises were that were getting louder.

"I'm here. What do you want?" Douglas hadn't a clue who the woman was that was standing across from him. But she was a fine-looking piece of ass, and he wondered if he'd already found—

"I'm your sister, dumbass. Get those thoughts out of your head right now."

"Nah, you can't be my sister. She's as ugly as sin." She sat down on the chair that he'd not noticed before now. "Is it really you, Carrie? I won't believe you even if you swear on a bible that it's you. Who are you, and what the hell are you doing here?"

"Your full name is Sherman Douglas Hunter. Our parents were Caroline and Peter Hunter. They've been gone for about five years or so now. They died about four days apart. You hired thugs by the name of Skank Eye and Whistle Stop to rob the restaurant where I was working at. They're both dead, as is Shelly Gibson. She died of—" He told her that he believed her now. "I'm so very glad. What is it you want with me? I'm going to start this off with me telling you that I'm not going to bail you out. I like you being here. Also, you have no bail set as you're in here because of the shit that you've pulled for so long and finally got caught at. Also, I'm not going to testify for you. I loath you as much as you do me, I suppose."

"I'm going to need some money when I get out of here. The best that I can figure, they only got me on some trumped-up charges about me hitting around Shelly or something. I wasn't the one that beat her to shit all the time. She did that on her own." Carrie just laughed and told him that he was also directly being charged with his buddies that came into the restaurant for the money."

"Right, like that's going to be believed. Nothing to do with me. They could have been hired by anyone but not me. What else? I'm sure that you have the low down on what they think they have on me." She told him that she wasn't his attorney but knew that they had a long list of things he'd done. "Nothing then. They have nothing on me, so I'll be getting out soon. As I was saying, I'm going to need some money. Someone said that you married one of the Sheppards. I don't care how you got him to put a ring on your finger, but you'll get some money from him for me. I'll need a couple of million to start out with. Then I'll figure out an amount monthly that I'm going to need when I get myself a place to stay and some staff. I'd forgotten how much I love having someone clean up after me. What do you know of my parent's house?"

She told him that they were her parents as well. "All right, if you insist, our parents. Though, I don't think you should be counted as you didn't live at home as long as I did. But I'm willing to allow you to buy me out. But I'm still going to be living there."

"They left everything to me." He nodded, asking her if she had a comedy routine she was heading up later because her delivery needed work. "No. I don't. However, I was left their things, including money and all the property that they had amassed while they were alive. Grannie, too, is leaving everything to me in her will. She is still around — thanks for telling me that she was dead, but I've gone to see her now, and she's going to be coming home with me."

"You think. And I want her in the nursing home where she can't cause any trouble. She's going around telling lies about me." Carrie told him that so far, the police have found out that she wasn't lying about his involvement in the murder of a few people around town. "See? That right there is why she should be put back there. She's going to make me trouble, and I don't have time to mess with her now."

"What else do you want, Douglas? I have shit that needs my attention, and I'm not getting that done sitting around here with you going over things that you already know about." Douglas told his sister that she would leave when he was good and ready for her to leave. "I don't know if you realize this or not, but I've not done what you wanted me to do for years. Also, I'm on this side of the bars, and you're not. So if I wanted to walk away, there isn't any way for you to stop me. You have ten minutes. After that, I'm leaving you to never return. Tell me, in simple terms, what it is you seem to be needing, what you want so I can tell you that it's not going to happen."

"You'd better watch yourself, Carrie. All kinds of things could happen to you and your husband if you don't mind me." She smiled at him. It wasn't anything that he had seen on her face before. In fact, it kind of scared him a bit. "You're going to help me or so help me. I'm going to find you and murder you and that husband of yours."

"I'm not at all worried about you, Douglas. Archie, my husband, is the leap leader to a bunch of jaguars. Also, as I'm sure that you've heard, there are five more of the Shepherds that have taken me under their paws and treat me as their sister. They love me too." He told her that she was too ugly to have anyone love her. "And when I got here, you were thinking that I was a fine piece of ass. Make up your mind. Not that it matters to me one way or another. You have five and a half minutes left. And I still don't know what it is you think I'm going to do for you."

"I told you. You're going to get me some money so that I can live a good life. And you're going to keep me supplied in money until such time as you die. And you will, if only for me to collect money off your dead ass when you pass over." He laughed when she stood up. "Sit your ass down, Carrie. I'm not nearly done with you. You're going to stay here until such time as we work out what amount I feel you should be giving me."

When Carrie left him sitting there, he could hear her laughter as she moved down the hall. He'd not gotten a chance to ask her about any payment, nor did he settle up on the amount that she was going to give him. He told himself that he wasn't entitled like he knew people would call him, but since she'd gotten all the money from their parents, though he really thought they were more his than hers as he'd been around them longer, she should want to help him out. It was the least she could have done, considering the fact that he'd been in jail all this time and could have been helping him easily.

He laid back on the cot, nervous about how much it was creaking and making noises. He thought about what she'd told him. It was then that he realized that she'd not had a ring on her finger. Not even a nice watch or something to prove that she was married into money.

"She's a stupid liar, is what she is." It tickled him to no end that she was trying her best to make herself out to be more than she was. Married? Not likely. She was also more than likely lying about the money, too. He'd never seen his parents spend anything more than they had to. Not to mention, they seemed to be struggling to make ends meet when he'd been home. Christ, his sister was worse than he was. "A fucking cunt liar."

The more he thought about what she'd told him, the funnier he thought that it was. He would have been informed about his parents having a will. He was sure of that. And the very fact that she thought that she could get away with saying they left her everything was wrong too. Why would they do that? Carrie wasn't all that much, and he was their firstborn. He should have had it all by default. As soon as his attorney showed up, he'd have to tell them he changed his mind and wanted one now, Douglas was going to have him look into the things about the wills. Also, to have his grandmother put back where he'd put her after they'd died and make sure that no one else could take her out again. Christ, the old buzzard, had been telling lies about him since he'd been a kid. Not really lies, he supposed, they were all true, but she'd been telling on him anyway.

It was nearly midnight when he could finally sleep. Pondering and plotting was something that he did a great deal and tonight hadn't been any different. The day of his court hearing was on Monday, two days from today so he was going to have to get himself an attorney so that he could collect what was rightfully his. And damn, Carrie for not telling him about it sooner.

Closing his eyes, he popped them back open when someone said his name. It was eerily said like they were trying to spoke him. Sitting up, when he could see the light coming down the hall, he yelled at whoever it was that he was trying to sleep and didn't appreciate them waking him up. As soon as the woman, a very beautiful woman, stood in front of his cell, he decided to ignore her over laying back in his bed and pretending to be asleep.

"I know that you're awake, dumbass. I've come to make you aware of a few things. My name is Sunny Sheppard. Your sister is now mine because we married brothers. Technically, we're not sisters, but I already think of her as mine." He asked her if she was stupid. "Stupid? No, I don't believe so. But I do have some information for you about the wills that your parents have left behind. It really is telling that you don't believe that they'd leave you out. When I found out how much they paid for attorney fees, greasing palms to keep you from prison, as well as paying someone to keep you safe, it's small wonder that they didn't leave you shit. If it had been left up to me, I would have let your ass rot in prison, but I didn't know you then, or I would have taken care that you were out of Carrie's life. Anyway, according to the wills, they paid out the ass for you to be on the outside instead of prison, and that was your inheritance."

"No. That's not the way inheritances work. When they die, I get their money. They can't charge me for doing what they should have been doing anyway. I was their responsibility to keep safe and not use the money that was to be left to me. You have it wrong." She asked him about Carrie. "What about her? It's not my fault that she was Ms. Goody Two Shoes. Carrie has always been a stick in the mud about having fun, and that's why I know that they didn't leave it all to her. Maybe half of it, maybe. But not it all. Not that it matters. I'm going to make her give it to me anyway. It's the least that she can do because she took her time getting my money to me."

"Well, you go on believing what you want. Also, I'm here to talk to you about Shelly. Did you know that she kept a diary? And that she wrote down in it every misdeed that the two of you ever did? It's been a lot of fun going over the notes that she left and finding the bodies. She even wrote down what you used to kill them with. Isn't that the nicest thing she could have done?" He told her that she had no rights to Shelly's private things. "Of course, I don't, silly. But you know who does?

The FBI. Also, you might want to think on this too, her ghost is talking to Carrie about some little things that you have too."

When she put up her pinky finger and wiggled it, he knew just what she was saying to him. It had been pointed out to him the same way by Shelly a couple of times when she was pissed off that he didn't have enough dick to satisfy even himself when he jerked off, he was so small. She'd even called him pencil dick too. One of those golfer pencils, she told him.

Standing up, telling her to come to him so that he could pound her head and then show her what a real dick looked like, she laughed and walked back down the hall toward where she'd come from. No amount of threatening her would make her come back and when the door slammed behind her, he let his temper go and pounded on the bars, his commode as well as the walls to burn his frustrations out.

~*~

Mikey didn't move around very much. It hurt to just blink his eyes right now. But his sister was there with him, her bed next to his so that they could hold hands. He noticed that she needed it as much as he did. The contact with each other. When the door opened to their room, he was sure it was his father coming back, but it was Jameson. He was smiling when he pulled a chair up to talk to him. Sissy was sleeping, having gotten some pain medication from the nurse a little while ago.

"There are several things that we need to talk about. I'm glad that your sister is sleeping. Even though she's younger than you, she will need to be made aware of a few things later. When she's better. All right?" He told Jameson that he was ready. "Ready? I guess that would be something that you'd feel like the way that you grew up. All right then. Your grandmother on your mother's side is going to take the two of you in. I'm sure you're aware that your mom is gone."

"Yes. I was too late to save her." Jameson told him that had he been there when she was killed, then he might well have been murdered as well, leaving Sissy all alone. "I guess so. But she was all the family that we had."

"As I said, you have a grandma that is going to take you in. Also, you have all of us that will be there for you. The reason that I'm here is that I'm going to represent you, I'm an attorney when the case is brought before the court. It will have to be done, even though he's dead, so that you and your sister can collect on the insurance that was taken out from when your biological father was killed. And Benson is the one that killed him." Mikey nodded, knowing all his life that Benson had had a part in his dad's death. Not what he'd done, but all the same, he knew that he'd been the one who had killed him. "You know anything else that I can look into for the two of you? So you understand, the sloth will pay your grandmother for raising the two of you. If she does anything wrong, not that I think she will, but if you have any trouble, you just come and find one of us, and we'll take care of things."

"Thank you. I didn't know I had a grandma so that will be new to us." Jameson said that he'd not known either until he spoke with Carrie. "She's a nice lady, you know? I like her a lot."

"So do I. She's very special to all of us, as is Sunny, Nash's mate." He said that she scared him. "To be honest with you, Mikey, she scares me as well. But I don't tell her that. I don't want to be hurt."

They both laughed and he realized that he

didn't hurt as much as he had before. Maybe it was because he knew things were going to be all right or that his bear was making it better. Either way, he was glad for the company that he had.

Jameson talked about the things that were going to happen to him and his sister. The sloth leader, Roger Mann, said that a fund was being set up for him and his sister to pay for them to go to college, too. That was the best news that he'd heard all his life. That he was going to be able to go to college. He loved school.

When the nurse came to check on him and Sissy, Jameson told her that he needed something for the pain. He was correct, he was hurting pretty badly, but he didn't think it was very nice of him to get the meds when he had company. Jameson told him that he was going to have to make sure that he didn't get too overwhelmed with the pain. He told him that Carrie had given them a bit of magic so that he and Sissy would heal quicker.

When he started to drift off, he remembered about his mom. Feeling his eyes, even though they were closed, fill with tears at how she was gone. She had been the best mother in the whole wide world, and he didn't know what he was going to do without her there for him and Sissy all the time. He was just going to have to make sure that his sister was safe now that he was the man of the house. He knew that it was a lot of responsibility for a ten-year-old, but he thought that he was up for it. Plus, he had the Shepherds to look to when he needed advice. He wasn't entirely sure what their grandma might do for them. Mikey was slightly untrusting of a lot of people and was worried that she'd be just like Benson had been—he decided right then and there that he wasn't going to call him dad anymore.

Drifting in and out of sleep, he woke up a couple of times when he had to go to the bathroom. His wounds weren't on his legs, so he figured that he could go on his own. He barely made it to the bathroom and had to call for help to get him back to bed. Mikey had never felt so weak in his life as he did right now.

Archie was in his room when he made his way to the toilet the second time. He had a pizza with him, a cheese on one half and a pepperoni on the other half. He ate the cheese side, and his sister ate most of the other side. He'd never had a hot pizza since he'd been a little boy. It was a treat that he loved a great deal.

"How are the two of you feeling?" The chocolate milk was another thing that he'd not had in a long time. Drinking half of it in one drink, he smiled at Archie when he told him that he had more milk if he needed it. He told the man that he was doing a lot better now. "Good. I have some news for you both that I think that you'll like to hear about. Your grandma is coming by tomorrow to talk to the two of you. She thought that the two of you were dead. That's what Benson told her. She's been grieving so much lately. She told me that she was so happy to have you both come and live with her. She really seems like a very nice lady. I think that you'll love staying with her."

He told them things that Jameson had told him about the college education as well as other things that would come to them as they were orphaned now. Sissy cried a little bit, but she stopped when Mikey hugged her.

"The house that you were living in when your father passed away and Benson moved into is going to be torn down and rebuilt. As soon as it's finished, the three of you will move into it. It's going to be bigger than the one before with each of you having your own rooms along with your grandma." Mikey hadn't had his own things before and told Mr. Archie that. "I know. You two have had a bad life for a long time and we're going to help you as much as we can. You won't have to worry about a lot of things, including not having enough to eat again. I swear if I have it, you two will as well. And your grandma is going to benefit from taking you in as well, so you don't have to worry about her."

Archie was true to his word and Mikey had all the milk, switching to white milk after dinner that he wanted. His sister wanted some juice and he thought it was odd that he had some of that in his bag as well. Not wanting to mess things up for them, he didn't voice his questions but enjoyed having a good hot meal, the first in a very long time.

After Archie left, promising them that he'd be there in the morning before his grandma showed up to make sure that things were all right between them. Mikey was a little afraid, not remembering his grandma all that much. But he was assured, several times by Archie that he and his sister were going to be in good hands. He hoped so. He'd hate to have all this taken away from him now. It was nice to have clean clothing on and food in his belly when he wanted it.

Dozing off, he thought about his mother and Benson. He'd been so mean to his mom that there were times that he wanted to kill him himself. Mikey had wanted to grow up fast so that he could be big enough to make Benson gone but he was also glad now that he didn't do anything stupid. What Carrie had told him when she'd come to visit him earlier. When his sister said his name, he looked over at her and smiled.

"Will we be all right, you think? I don't want to go anywhere anymore if people are going to hurt us. Do you?" He told her what Archie had said. "I know that people have different faces, Mikey. One that they show the people from the welfare and the one that they show us. I'm worried that our grandma has been showing them the other face and that when we go and live with her, she's going to be like Benson."

"Don't you remember her from when you were little?" Sissy told him that she didn't remember her at all. "Well, I remember some of her. Christmases were so nice. There was so much food on the table that I nearly burst. She had so many different kinds of cookies and cakes. I just remembered what she told me once. That Christmas was for sweets, and Thanksgiving was for food. I forgot about that."

He grinned, holding his sister's hand while he told her of other stories that he was just remembering about grandma. The one about his grandpa, who he'd forgotten about until then, made the two of them laugh.

"Grandda used to read the Christmas story to us. He held you in his lap, and you just stared at him like he was speaking right to you. He might have been, now that I think on it." She laughed asking him to tell the story to her again. "We'd lay out cookies and milk for Santa, too. He even had some carrots that he put into storage that still had the tops on them. He told me once that the reindeer loved the tops more than the carrots themselves."

Mikey had long since given up his belief in Santa. It was mostly because Benson had told him he was a baby for believing in him. But he'd keep believing if he could see how happy it made his little sister to believe.

"He'd sing with us too. I never told him, but

he was a terrible singer. But he did it with gusto, as mom used to say. I was so sad when he passed away. He'd been really old, in his fifties, but he had a bad heart that nobody knew about, and it took him from us." Mikey was going to tell his sister stories about their mom, too, things that had to do with before Benson came into their lives. His dad, too. So she'd know what awesome people they were. "Dad was the only one besides Grandma that would eat pecan pie. I don't remember if I got to try it, but Dad would be sick the next day for eating too much of it. He'd swear that he wasn't going to eat it again, only to eat it again the next year. He was funny like that."

Mikey told his sister about birthdays, his and hers, until he was too tired to speak. Sissy had been asleep for a few minutes when he finally thought that he could sleep too. Closing his eyes, he let rest take him under and hoped that he didn't have any bad dreams tonight. Mikey couldn't believe how much better he felt, just talking about the family with Sissy than he had in a very long time. He decided that he was going to get him a notebook and write some of the things down that he remembered so that he could share them with his sister. And her kids, if she had any. Mikey didn't think he'd ever have children. Benson had told him that he was just too stupid and ugly to have a mate.

His dreams had always been nightmares. Tonight, it started out with the same dream he'd had every night since being in the hospital. It was his mother being dead and Benson trying to kill him. It was all out of order this time, but he saw things that he'd not remembered before. Like his mom telling him how much she loved him and Sissy as she hid away from Benson. How sorry she was that she'd not been able to protect them better. There were other things, too, good things like the stories that he told his sister that he'd loved. Mikey finally felt at rest when his mom, as she used to do before Benson, kissed him on the forehead and told him that he was the best little boy in the world. Rolling to his side, he remembered believing her and he wanted to be able to remember things like that all the time.

Chapter 6

Carrie thought that the entire town had turned out for the trial for her brother. It was just as well, she thought. Carrie thought that there wasn't a single person in town who hadn't been hurt by some of the actions of her brother. Some of them more than she had. Once the judge, the honorable Judge Harold J. Cutthroat, was seated, a very fitting name from what she'd heard, things were called to order. Since this was the only thing he had on his calendar today, he told everyone in the room he was willing, if they were to not read the charges against Douglas, to forego the reading of the list of charges that had been brought before the courts concerning Douglas. Of course, he stood up and disagreed.

"You want to know what you're being tried for, young man? I would have thought that with you requesting an attorney at the last minute, you would have had a pretty good idea why the state is wanting a piece of you about. By the way, Mr. Lockheart had been calling me every hour, trying to get out of representing you. What have you been doing to him?" He said that she was a girl, not a man. "According to my paperwork, Mr. Terry Lockheart is a transgender male. Remember that in the future. What have you done to him?"

"Why isn't anyone just what they seem to be?" Douglas waved his hands in dismissal. "Regardless. I don't want whatever it is to be working for me. She…it wants me to plead guilty to all the charges. Saying something about a lesser sentence. I don't know what you have on me, and frankly, I don't care, but it's not enough for me to have to go to prison for. Just tell me what my bail is going to be so my sister can pay it off. Then, I'd like to get to the real reason that I agreed to come here today. She told me that everything from my parents was left to her. She's a liar. There isn't any way that my parents would have done that to me. I'm their son and the firstborn. That's the way things work."

"All right. I'm willing to address your concerns first. I have nothing to do today, so let's get right to that. I've seen your parents will. Your sister's attorney was kind enough to make sure I had a copy. There is no mention of you at all in their will. A couple of charities, a perpetual grant for their graves, and your sister. Mrs. Sheppard was to get everything, including any and all insurance policies that were in their names as well as any and all properties that they owned." He put down the will and looked at Douglas. "There you see? Nothing for you. Not even a mention that you were even their son. I do know, too, that there was a letter that was given to you a few days after the funeral from your parents. I have a copy of that as well. Did you read it?"

"I don't remember a letter of any kind. I told you that she was a liar. It's probably saying that it was all a joke and that Carrie doesn't get shit." He was told to watch his language. "Whatever. If I have to pay a fine or whatever, just keep track of it, and my sister will pay. It's the least that she can do since she kept me from having any kind of fun after they passed away. Also, she needs to put that old broad back in the nursing home."

"You mean your grandmother." Douglas told the judge that she was telling lies on him, too, and he wasn't going to have it. "Well, I'm sorry to burst your bubble, Douglas, but you have no say over where your grandmother lives. From what I'm to understand, she's going to be staying with your sister to live out her life. Again, nothing to do with you."

"You're not listening to me. Is there someone else that can be in your spot? You're only acting on things that are in favor of Carrie. That's not going to get me out of here and the money that she owes me." Jameson handed the judge a file, and she waited for Douglas to get mad again. "What's that? Something that I need to know about?"

"It says here that you were given the letter from your parents twenty-four hours after they were buried. You signed for it. Before you tell me that you didn't, I have a picture of you being handed it and your signature you put to the paperwork to verify that you received it. If you read it, then you know as well as I do that they didn't leave you anything because they'd been bailing you out for years. Also, and this one I find terribly disturbing, they'd been paying people off that you hurt so that they'd not sue you as they wanted to do. It says here in their letter to you that it was well over several million dollars they paid out. What do you have to say about that?"

"So? It's not as if they didn't have it. So, I don't understand what their beef is. I'm their son, and they had to know that one day, I'd take over their money. And as for paying people not to sue me, that's their job. As their son, they're responsible for me and my actions." Carrie laughed and had the judge and Douglas turning to her. "What the hell do you find so funny? You took my money, and I'm going to get it back. Also, you're going to pay me once a month too so that I can live the life that I want to. We never got to finalize that when you came to see me the other day."

Jameson spoke up, saying that he had a transcript about their conversation at the jail. Again, Douglas objected to someone doing something that he'd not allowed but was ignored for the most part. The judge said that he'd read it over and knew exactly what had been said between the two of them. Douglas was red hot in his anger. He asked him why he was just now getting around to reading it.

"I'm just now being informed about it. Shut your trap and sit down. The longer you keep yapping at me the longer this is going to take for me to read. Mrs. Sheppard? Can you verify that this is correct that your brother threatened you?" Carrie said it wasn't the first time he'd done that. "I have no doubt about that whatsoever." He turned to Douglas. "You don't have a single cell in your body that makes me think that you're the least bit nice. No wonder your parents didn't leave you anything. I would have been hard-pressed to do that too if I were in their boots."

"Then I guess it's a good thing that you're not." Douglas huffed. "Okay, so I got the letter and read it. So? It's not like I believed it. Or, for that matter, thought about how it was going to affect me. The stupid thing said that as soon as I was given that letter, then the will would be read. I wasn't notified, so I didn't believe that it had been. It didn't count if I wasn't there. I also didn't want to believe that my sister and parents would cut me off so violently. To leave me nothing is not the way things are supposed to be done. I was their son, their oldest, and I should have been left everything. I might well have been all right with splitting it with Carrie, but no more. I want it all, and I plan on getting it even if I have to take her out of the picture."

"So you've said. You're willing to murder your sister and her husband because of money, is that right?" Douglas told the judge that it would be totally up to them if he had to murder them, as well as their fault if he ended up having to do it. "You're very entitled, aren't you, Douglas? You think that everything should be handed to you on a silver platter, no doubt as well."

"No. I'd rather have gold, but no, a platter isn't necessary at all. Small bills would be better than—no strike that. I'd rather have large ones. A bunch of small ones would clutter up my wallet. Or even an endless spending credit card. As I told my sister, since I have no idea what my needs will be, now that I think on it, a credit card would be much better. Wouldn't you agree?" Judge Cutthroat looked at her before asking Douglas if he had anything else that he wanted to share with the courtroom. "Of course. I don't know where Carrie is living with her 'supposed' husband but they'll need to make sure that my home is better, bigger too. Also, I'm going to need a staff. That's not entitlement, just something that I'm used to having and have been missing from my life recently. Just because she's a liar doesn't mean that I should be doing without."

"No, we couldn't have that, could we?" Judge Cutthroat asked him again what his demands were. Douglas assured him that they weren't demands but things that he was supposed to have had all along. "Even though you weren't left anything by your parents, you still feel that you should have gotten their estate. Is that what you're saying?"

"It's not my fault that they're not here to make things right. I mean, I didn't kill them off. Had I known their plans for me or their supposed plans for me, I would have made them see reason. I would never have allowed them to get away with cutting me out of everything. Never." She stood up and asked him what he meant by that. All rules, it seemed, had gone out the window a long time ago today and she wanted answers too. "Carrie, Carrie, Carrie. What do you think that I meant? I would have forced their hand and made sure that I was left with everything. Then I would have had to dispose of them, not kill, just would have gotten rid of them so that they'd have no chance of going behind my back—much like they did now and change the will to be in your favor. Then I would have taken care that you weren't able to collect. That might have been easier in the first place, but I didn't think they had it in them to leave me out of the will. I should have known that beforehand so that I could have stopped it from happening."

"That sounds like you would have killed them. I don't know your definition of dispose of, but it does sound to me like you would have ended their lives." He shrugged at her. When Jameson told her to keep talking to her brother through their link, talking about what his plans were, she realized something she'd not before. Douglas was confessing to a great many things that needed to be put out there. "And you would have killed me as well. You said that to me. That you would kill myself and my husband when you got out. Is that still something that you wish to do."

"Not wish to do. I have to do it. Once I get this all cleared up, I don't want you going behind my back and having me arrested again. You did that, didn't you? They told me that Shelly had spoken to you before she died. She hated you, why would she go to you without my permission. That's just it. She wouldn't have. Never. I knocked her around, sure. But I didn't kill her. Mores the pity. However, she's thankfully dead, so I don't have to worry about her sharing what I'm going to be making any longer." She told him he was cold. "No, I'm not. I'm a realist. I have a plan and I know that in order to make my plans come out the way that I want them to, I have to knock a few heads around. If they end up dying, great. One less thing that I have to worry about. You have your will made out, sister? When your husband is dead and gone along with you, you know who will inherit your estate, if I don't have it all already, it will be me."

Douglas laughed. It didn't sound maniacal. His face took on a look that looked serine to her. Normal. Like this was the man that she'd been around her entire life. She didn't know if he was insane or not. But she'd bet right now that there was something wrong with her brother. It caused her to shiver and the hairs on her neck and arms to stand up. When he turned back to the judge to speak to him about being freed as he'd had things to take care of, Carrie looked around the room.

There were at least a dozen ghosts there and they'd all had their heads bashed in. She knew at that moment that Douglas had killed each and every one of them by doing just what he'd done to Shelly. She now believed every entry in the other woman's diary that told of the people that had disappeared, and she knew too that it really had been by her brother's hand. She wondered for the first time if her brother had been killing people all his life. That would explain why these ghosts weren't in the diary that Shelly had kept. Walking to Jameson, she picked up his pen and using his pad of paper, began writing down the names of each of the people in the room. They also gave her their date of death, along with the reason that Douglas had killed them.

Sixteen people. Sixteen men and women that had been murdered because they'd denied Douglas something that he'd wanted. A haircut that hadn't been right. Dry cleaning that had left a stain of blood on a shirt that he'd dropped off bloodied and dirty. A ticket for his parking in a no-parking zone. All of them small in comparison to them dying for them. When the last of them had given her their name and date of death, Carrie began reading their names, telling everyone in the room what they'd done in order to have their lives taken from them and their families.

"George Ridgeway, seventy-eight, died in April fifteen years ago because he'd accidentally fallen against Douglas's car when he tripped over a bad place in the sidewalk. He had his head bashed in by a piece of concrete that Douglas picked up from the sidewalk. Sharon James, twenty-two, died that same month when her baby cried out in its stroller, startling Douglas enough to make him jump. Douglas killed her because she didn't say she was sorry to him quickly enough. She was comforting her baby instead of comforting a grown assed man." She named them all, ending with the death of a little boy from down the street. "Bill Warner, seven, had tossed a ball at Douglas when he'd asked him to. Then he laughed when Douglas had missed it. The boy had not just his head smashed in, but Douglas had stripped him naked before tossing him into the lake behind the boy's home. Age nor the reason made any difference to Douglas. If you were in his way, did something he found offensive, or just laughed, he would kill you if the mood struck him. And I'm sure, as the weeks go on, there will be more deaths that we find that their deaths are somehow, petty no doubt killed by Douglas."

"You can't be bringing those up now, dumbass. They were when I was a kid and those records had been sealed. Christ, you're a dumbass." The judge turned to his bailiff and whispered something to him. "I demand that you tell me what you're talking about. I won't have you keeping secrets from me. If this, whatever you're saying, pertains to me, then I deserve to know it."

"I'm having your records unsealed and brought to me. I'd like to see what sort of things that someone thought shouldn't be out in the open about your personality. Also, since you brought it up, I want to have them for today. Thank you for that." Douglas complained about having his records unearthed, saying it was a breach in contract—whatever the hell that meant and that it would hurt him if someone were to read them over. "Well, now, this might turn out better than I thought. Yes, I can't wait to read about things that a younger Douglas would do then sealed away."

When the bailiff returned, he wasn't alone.

Not only did two more men follow him into the courtroom, but the three of them were carrying two boxes, each filled with what appeared to be files. Judge Cutthroat looked about as shocked as Carrie felt. Six boxes of deeds that had been committed by her brother before he'd turned eighteen. This couldn't be good, she thought. It was too much.

"I see that you've been very busy, Douglas. My goodness." The judge, leaving his seat in favor of having the boxes set on the table that had been brought out too, pulled the lid off of one of the boxes and pulled out a random file. "This is the Bill Warner file. A seven-year-old boy had been playing kickball with some of his friends. Douglas was there too and asked young Bill if he would toss the ball to him. It says here that witnesses thought that Douglas was going to cut the ball, deflating it but he put the ball down on the ground and looked like he was going to kick it hard. But in his exuberance to kick it, he missed, falling onto the ground, and the ball laid where it was. All of the children laughed then Bill asked to have the ball back." He read the rest to himself. "It says here that you threatened each of the kids that you were going to kill them, but Bill didn't run as quickly as the others and was caught by him."

"He never laughed at me again, by god." Douglas sounded proud of the fact that he'd killed an innocent boy. "None of the others would hang around when I was in town either. I didn't get to play ball with them, but I believe I enjoyed them being afraid of me more. Come on, read another one. This is like a good walk down memory lane for me."

She could tell that the judge didn't want to read anything else from the file. It sort of sickened her, too, that he was acting like this mattered little to him. But the judge pulled another file out and handed it to Jameson. When he stood up, he looked at Douglas before opening the file.

"Douglas Hunter, age twelve, confessed to killing Ewing Gibson, age twenty. They had a disagreement over seating in the movie theater. Mr. Hunter wanted to sit in the very middle of the theater without anyone around him. He had wanted to have the row directly behind him, in front of him, and the one that he was seated in emptied so that he could enjoy the movie by spreading out. As the theater was full, a first showing of a brand new movie, Gibson had sat in the row in front of Hunter with his date, Margret Jane." Douglas laughed and told Jameson to go on. It was a delightful story. "When he wouldn't move away, Hunter broke the arm off the seat he was sitting next to and beat both Gibson and Jane to death."

Douglas laughed. "He thought that he should have had the seats that I wanted. I had to teach them both a lesson in crossing me. It's always been so that I got what I wanted. I have no idea why this man and his girlfriend thought that they'd be some kind of exception to the rules that I had." He shook his head and looked at her. "Carrie, you remember that, don't you? You weren't allowed to sit next to me because I needed what I wanted."

"No. I knew better than to be anywhere you were. Even at home, I wouldn't be in the same room as you were. You were dangerous to me even when I was just a toddler." He nodded again, laughing hard at some kind of joke that only he understood. "You've been a bastard all your life, haven't you? You killed for the sake of killing. You should be locked up."

"Locked up? Not unless they were to put me in a cell all to myself with only a hole to get my food

from. I'd kill anything that came to me right away."
He turned to the judge before speaking again. "She
thinks I'm dangerous. That's not it at all. I'm a man
that likes to have things my way. I don't believe
I should ever have to compromise. Why should
I? Things are there for me, and I should and will
take them when I want them. Everyone should
understand that about me. I mean, look how many
times I had to teach someone that lesson."

Douglas pointed to the file boxes and then
looked at her. Before he could speak, if that was
what he was going to do, she didn't take her eyes
off him when she told him that he needed to be
dead rather than locked away. She thought that
the world would be better off if he wasn't in it.

"Oh, Carrie. When will you learn that people
like me don't die? We keep making rules that you
have to follow all the time. And if you get in the
way? Well, I guess that you'd end up in a file just
like the other people who crossed me did."

Carrie left the courtroom. She could no
longer stand to be in the same room as her brother.
The very air around him stank. He was evil, and
she was sure that if he ever got out, he'd test their
immortality to the limit. Or he'd find someway of

killing them that hadn't been made up as yet. Her brother was—

Running to the corner of the building, she threw up several times when she thought of the people who had been in the courtroom that he'd killed. People who had lives. Children that hadn't gotten to grow up. Her heart ached for everyone that he'd killed and wished that she could have done something about him when they'd been younger. Or, at the very least, her parents should have done something to have him examined so he'd be someplace safe for all humanity.

"Are you all right?" She told Archie that she wasn't and didn't think she would be ever again so long as Douglas was around. *"The judge is taking a quick break, but he had Douglas chained to the floor before doing so. As you can imagine, he's not at all happy about it. An officer held a gun to his head while they chained his wrists. Then his legs, too. I don't think any of them wanted to be that close to him to do it."*

"No, I don't think that I would have either." She looked at the Dari Twist, the ice cream and soda shop across from the courthouse. *"I'm going to go and have a banana split for myself. Then I'm going to walk home. If you want to join me, I'm not sharing. I*

need this more than my next breath."

"I understand completely. I'm going to stay in here in the event that Jameson needs me. Also, I can keep an eye on him too. He's about as shell-shocked as anyone that I've ever seen. I have to admit, this is about the strangest court hearing that I've ever been to. Even if it had been my own mother, I wouldn't have believed it without being here." They both laughed. *"You enjoy your split and I'll talk to you again when things are settled up. I believe that the judge is going to put him away, but it's hard to tell right now. Poor man."*

Carrie did enjoy her ice cream. Just as she was digging into the second scoop of chocolate-covered ice cream, Mikey came to sit with her. He smiled a huge smile and showed her his new shoes as well as the hat he'd gotten. It took his sister a little bit longer to get to them. She and their grandma were admiring the flowers in the barrel next to the small shop. Also, Sissy was in a wheelchair still and wasn't getting around as well as her brother.

"We came to have some ice cream, too. Grannie said that we've been so good that we all deserved a treat. I love her." Carrie gave him the rest of her ice cream, having had too much as it was, and he ate it while telling her everything that the three of them had been up to. "Grannie also told us that she's got nothing to go back to, so she's going to be looking for a house around here. I'm glad. The sloth is taking good care of us, and I like having my friends around. I've made so many of them now."

"I bet you have." Grannie, Ms. Granger sat down while Mikey went up and got their order for them. "How are you doing? The kids are all right, aren't they?"

"Oh yes. Oh my, they're the best little kids. I love having them around." She looked at them with so much love that Carrie felt it in her soul. "Mikey has been especially helpful with his sister. I sometimes…well, I wasn't in a good place before coming here. I missed my family. My daughter and I had very little to do with each other after she met that man. But these two have brought me back to life, it almost seems, and I am grateful for them every day."

They spoke about things that the sloth was giving them. Ms. Granger was a bear, too, and she was enjoying having a good leader over the one that she'd had before. Carrie mentioned that she and Archie were the leap leaders, and she seemed very happy about that. Ms. Granger asked if she knew anything about the local schools.

"Not too much, I'm afraid. Mikey and his sister would know more, I'm sure. We've been invited to allow our kids to go to the pack school when we have any. We're keeping our options open. We've only been together for a few weeks so far." She said that she noticed that the leap had a lot of things going on in town. "Yes. Improvements to help out the town. Taking care of a few things too that might bring in a few new businesses."

"My son. Oh, I'm so happy you brought that up. Larence Granger, he's my son had a huge car shop. He not only sells some used cars, but he has a lot of men who work for him that do repairs, too. He's looking for a place with a good deal of land. He wishes to sell some new cars too. Oh, what an enterprise he has for his family. He helps out with my bills, too, every month. He'd probably enjoy having to move here to be closer to myself and the kids." She asked a few questions, not really sure what it would take to have a business to move in. "I can have him give you a call if he's wanting to do that. Wouldn't that be really nice? I know that he employs quite a few people, over a dozen of them."

She didn't even know if that was a lot of people but it would be twelve more people with an income. If he sold cars, too, there is no telling how many more would be working. Talking to her and making notes, not wanting to bother the men just yet—she wanted them to be on their toes around Douglas—so she wrote down as much as she could about some of the questions that she, as well as Ms. Granger, had.

In her excitement, Carrie almost forgot all about her brother and the shit that he was pulling. It felt good, too, to think that she might help out the town by helping bring a business to town, too. If only that would be that easy.

After the older woman left, telling her that the kids had some chores to do, Carrie was happy to see that the kids didn't seem to mind at all about working for their meals. All they were doing today was snapping green beans for their dinner and shucking corn. That made her mouth water for both those foods, and wondered if their cook could make that for dinner one night. She especially loved fried green tomatoes, another treat that the kids were going to have for dinner, and wanted to beg to go home with them. But she didn't, as tempting as it had been.

Chapter 7

Carrie was seated in a large room with plants around her. She'd discovered, quite by accident, that when there were a lot of ghosts around, the air seemed stale and tainted. She didn't want to say it was because they were dead, but it stood to reason that was it. Lifting her head up when the first ghost came into the room, Carrie smiled and asked her if she'd had any trouble getting there.

"No. It was fine. I would, however, like to suggest a change in the way you have us come in. I think that there should be days for a certain kind of people. Then, another day for others. Also, you shouldn't have us all in one room like cattle. It's a bit difficult for folks like myself to want to see you if there is an unwashed air to the place."

The woman looked at the chairs, knowing full well whether she could sit or not. It didn't matter what she had in the room. "I suppose this is all you have? Or is this just what you had lying around before you got the good stuff brought in."

She didn't want to start her day off like this but that was the job that she had. Asking for information about herself, the woman finally sat down on something that was on her end and looked to be floating in the air on hers. Carrie didn't care. It was her first day of having a scheduled time, and she was going to make the most of it. If she could.

"What complaint do you have that I'm willing to help you with. If you're here to have me change things to suit yourself on either side, you're out of luck. I won't, and I can't." Dana asked her which side she wouldn't. "Mine. Now, what is it you want? I have a very busy day, and if you don't have something to talk to me about, then let's move on."

"It's my daughter-in-law, Diana. I don't know why her parents gave her such a regal name when—" Carrie told her that she wasn't going to listen to her go on about things that wouldn't be changed just to suit her. "All right then. I want you to let me go back and take care of her and that child she brought to the marriage. Why my son married her is—" All she did was raise her hand. "I want her out of his life. She's a bad influence on him and gets him into trouble all the time. She needs for me to go there and take care of her. Christ, you do make this difficult, don't you?"

"Don't care. Now, this daughter-in-law? Is this the one that you accused of stealing your watch? The very one that you have on now?" She tried to hide the watch with her sleeve, but it wasn't happening. "I'm going to take that as a yes. Diana has been a good and loving wife to your son, Carter. The child in question…it says here that it's your son's child from when they were lovers in high—"

"What a disgusting word, lovers. She seduced him so that she could get at my money." Carrie was so happy for the hyped-up computer that Sunny had made for her. All she had to do was put in a name, and it gave her everything that they'd ever done. Even the dead, when necessary, she had information on them that more than likely they didn't know about themselves. "I don't believe for a moment that that thing is my son's child."

"Again, I don't care. She's his, and that's all there is to it. If it makes you feel any better, they had DNA tests…Ah, I see. You knew about that but still didn't believe it. That's really too bad on your part. But nothing to do with you being a ghost. You're not going to harm either the child, who is very intelligent, by the way, or your wonderful daughter-in-law. It says here that she gave up her job to take care of you after you had your stroke. I see also that you treated her terribly, spitting at her and pissing the bed when you were able to get up and use the potty. Shame on you. So now that we've established that you're not a nice person and that you're not going to be able to go back to doing whatever you have in your sick mind, is there anything else that I can help you with? Or better yet, tell you, no, you're not going to do it?"

"You're not at all what I want. Is there someone who is a better servant to us? Someone perhaps a little older?" Carrie just stared at her without answering. There wasn't anyone else, as a matter of fact, unless she wanted to go across the earth to find one. "Well?"

"Well, what?" She was so frustrated that she

faded out and in for a few seconds. It took a great deal of energy to be pissed off, Carrie knew, and it didn't bother her in the least bit that the woman was mad at her. "If there is nothing else, I think your time is up."

"I didn't get my request settled up. You can't just toss me away like I'm nothing. I demand to be able to take care of her and that child." Carrie stood up, and the woman either didn't care or didn't know that she'd pissed her off now. "What now? Are you going to send me away? You can't do that either. I know my rights."

The woman simply disappeared. Carrie asked who was next and when the little man, she knew that he'd been in his late nineties when he'd passed away, she asked him what he needed. The man smiled and then laughed. She didn't know what was going on until he finally started to speak.

"I don't have any family left, my dear. Would it be all right if I were to sit in the corner, I won't make a sound, to watch you work? I tell you, I've been wanting someone to take care of that woman for months. She did nothing but berate that poor child and her mother to all of us. I think her daughter-in-law is lucky that she passed when she did. There is no telling what sort of things she would have done to her had she been around." She told him that would be up to the people that came into the room. "Fine, fine. I'm harmless. I'm thinking that I won't have any trouble from now on. I'll gladly leave if they wish. But I'm grateful if they do. I had a very boring life, you see."

Throughout the rest of the day, Mr. Abers was allowed to stay in the room while conducting business. She only ran into one other person that had it in his head that he was in charge but she quickly turned him around and sent him on his way. Not away, but back to the waiting room. She was happy that she was getting better at dealing with people this way, and having a schedule meant that she could leave at the end of the day and not return until the next day. She didn't know how anyone else did this but she was happy for the free time that she had.

On her way home, she noticed something that she'd not before. There were ghosts all over the town. Some of them were very old ghosts from a time so long ago that she wondered what the town had looked like back in the day. She also noticed that there were several high school kids, some younger ones, too, that hung around the Dari Twist. A favorite haunt of all ages it appeared. Carrie thought that it had to do with all the children that were there, laughing and having a wonderful time sharing ice cream with one another.

"Ms. Sheppard?" It startled her at times when someone called her that. This time was no different. Turning to speak to the man, she backed away from him when she realized that he was carrying a weapon and that she didn't know him. "Don't make any kind of sudden moves. I've been set to find you for some time now, and I would hate to have to kill you before I get you to my boss."

"What boss could you possibly have that would have you taking me at knifepoint in front of about three dozen people?" She looked around, and he did, too. Taking that time to slap the knife out of his hand, he stood there staring at her like she was some kind of oddity. "Well, where are we going? I don't mind going with you had you only asked. But having a knife sort of puts me off. Next time someone sends you after someone, see if they're all right with following you. All right?" He nodded. "Use your words. Nodding is rude unless you have an ailment that keeps you from speaking."

"Yes, ma'am. I'll do...he told me that I might have to knock you around a bit before you see things his way. I didn't much want to do this, but he forced my hand, leaving me no choice." She told him that everyone had a choice in everything they did. "Not with this guy. As you might have guessed, it's your brother. He said that you've been treating him poorly and that you owe him a great deal of money. I want my family back, you see. And I won't get them until I bring you to him."

"Have you checked with your family? Are they really missing?" He nodded again then told her that he'd been trying to reach them for several days now. "All right. I'll see what I can do to find them for you. I'm sorry to tell you, but if Douglas has something to do with your family missing, he might well have already had them murdered. He's not the most reliable person, and he's been killing people for a very long time. Let me check for you."

After getting the man's name and that of his wife, she called out to her, hoping that she'd not come to her, that would indicate that she was still alive. When she arrived where the two of them were standing, Carrie could have cried. She told

Matthew that she was indeed gone then he asked about his children.

"They're with my mother, miss." She told Matthew where his girls were and that his wife said that she'd taken them to her home that morning so that she could get the house in order. "I don't think that the man who came for us knew about the children. But my mom, she will have the recordings of him coming into the house. Matt and I set up cameras all over the house so that we could keep a good eye on our little ones. I hope she was able to get them from the cloud."

Going to the police department with Matthew in tow, she spoke to Larry, the man who knew what sort of things she could do, and told him about the Sayer family. He sent a cruiser over to the house and one to her mother's house to check on the children—a welfare check, so to speak. Once they were gone, he took her into a room after asking to speak to her.

"I have three missing teenagers. Their parents are going crazy thinking the worst. If you could...I don't know, do your thing and find them for me, I'd be much obliged. They've been missing for two days now and we've no sign of them at all around here. Please?" She asked the things that she needed to know to call out to them, and only one of them came to her. Larry asked if the others were hurt. "I can go and get them myself, even though I'm acting chief right now while Denny is on his vacation. I honestly don't think that the man is returning, but that could just be me. I don't know that I would with all the crap that he had going on."

She'd heard about the police chief and that he'd been gambling heavily before being asked to take some time off without pay. She didn't think he'd come back either, but then she never thought to be talking to ghosts either.

Carrie reached out to Archie, knowing that wherever he was, he'd be there for her. She told him everything that she had going on, and he said that he'd meet her at the jail. Telling him that she would be so happy about that, Carrie and Matthew waited until he came to see them. The poor man was grief-stricken, to say the least. Her heart broke for him.

The jail wasn't busy today, and they were able to see Douglas, with an armed guard, of course, while he was still in his cell. She'd never seen her brother so disheveled before and was surprised to hear him talking to the walls. When she made herself known to him, he turned and looked at her, then spit. It didn't reach her, of course, but she pretended that it didn't bother her at all, even though she was sickened by his apparent disregard for anything she had to say to him.

"What the fuck do you want? If you haven't come here to tell me that I'm getting out, then you might as well go fuck yourself. I have nothing to say to you otherwise." She said that the police were at the house of Maggie and Matt Sayer. "I don't know what you're talking about. I said for you to go away. As I said, unless—"

"We know that you had her killed, and we have it on a recording. After talking to the man you hired, he's spilled the beans on what you wanted and the fact that you were going to pay him ten grand when you were set free. I don't know how you planned on paying him even a dime, Douglas, you don't have shit to bargain with." He told her that he would when she got off her ass and gave him the money. "When are you going to get it through your thick head that you're getting nothing? You're headed to prison in the morning, and there you will die. I'm not going to support anything that you need. No money in your fund. You'll live as a pauper, and you'll die one too, being buried on the very land that you spend the rest of your life at."

"You slut." She forgot that Archie was with her until Douglas went flying back against the wall behind him with his face smashed up and bloodied. Smiling at Archie, she kissed him on the mouth quickly and waited for Douglas to either die or get up. Either way, she wasn't going to take his crap anymore.

Douglas stood up. She was pissed off that he'd not just died then and told her that he was going to get her. Carrie wasn't worried and told him so as she gathered up the men with her and left the long hall. She could hear Douglas bitching about her leaving without his permission even as she exited the doorway and made her way to the outdoors. Archie was helping Matthew with his grief as they took him to his home.

~*~

"He's going to be taken to prison at four in the morning. We're hoping that getting him up at an ungodly hour that he'll be less pissy. I don't think that is possible, but I don't know." Archie asked Larry if he needed any help. "I'm glad that you asked. If you could maybe spare a few of your jags to surround him while being taken out, that would be good. I'm going to go so far as to tell you that if he gets out of line, even a little, they have my permission to take him out. I don't think that he'll last long in prison anyway *if* he makes it there."

"I can do that." Larry cautioned him about using his family. "I never thought of that, but I can see where that might be an issue. No, I'll get some men and women that he's dealt with before. That'll put them on their toes, so to speak." Larry asked where Carrie was. "She's doing some search on your missing teenagers. Do you know the parents very well?"

"Why? Did something happen that is going to make me have to look harder at them?" Archie nodded, telling him that so far, she'd been able to find one of the boys. Then told him how his parents were involved in the fact that they were missing. "You say that they provided them with alcohol? They made it sound like they were the purest kids that ever walked the earth. How much did they give them? And where did he get it for them?"

"Locally. He gave them several cases of beer as well as some wine. Carrie said that it looks like they started out at the barn, the one out there on forty, and that's where she found the Stable boy. The other three she's still looking for. Carrie said that they might not realize that they're dead yet, or they're not. But it's been hard to find them." Larry told him that any help would be more than he had now. "I heard that Mr. Carolle is complaining that you're not doing enough to find the kids. Also that they'd better not be dead, or he's going to be suing the department for their lack of help. Once it comes out that he and the others were supplying alcohol for them, they'll be run out of town on a rail."

"Wouldn't bother me one bit if they are. All they do is bitch and complain about how the police are worthless. I guess three weeks ago, he'd had his mailbox busted off. I don't know for sure, but I think one of the elders of the town did it in the middle of the night with his bulldozer." Archie asked why he'd do that. "First of all, it's too low to the ground. Makes it hard for the mail carrier to deliver the mail with it being lower than their window. Also, did you know that it's against the law to have your box so that it's not a breakaway support? Yeah. It can't be set in any kind of concrete that will have it standing if hit by a car or other obstacle. Thus, the reason for the bulldozer. I heard tell that he was making this one harder to hit as well as too high for the driver to get to. That'll be all right since I know that the Mail Service has informed him that he will not get his mail delivered to him if he doesn't comply with the rules. Kind of funny if you ask me. What the fuck is wrong with some people, I ask you, Archie? I think they get meaner daily, I do."

"I have to agree with you there." He told him about the woman that Carrie had to deal with. "I was sort of jealous of her having that power. But after a couple of stories about what she has to deal with, I'm glad that I don't. But she's really good at just sending them away now. No one messes with my wife."

The two of them talked about a couple of other things that Archie was going to look into for him. There was also the fund raiser that was coming up for the jail. Not only did they need an entirely new jail, but it wouldn't hurt if they were to have a few extras for the officers, too. Like bulletproof vests that were younger than he was. Guns and ammo as well. Most of the officers were supplying their own weapons and ammo, and they were having trouble with that as well. When Carrie showed up, he could tell that she was upset. At what? He had no idea, but he would bet anything that it had to do with the kids that she'd been looking for. When she spoke to Larry about the kids, he nearly laughed when she said that the kids were all gone and thinking that it was some lark that their dads had pulled on them.

"How would they think that their fathers could make them be dead only to bring them back when the joke was over? I tell you, if I ever have children, I'm going to lock them up away from other kids who might be as stupid as these three are. Christ." He did laugh then, and she glared at him. "What would you have said to them had they asked you—several hundred times, I might add, when they were going to be *alive* again. What does that even mean?"

"I don't know, love, but I'm sure they'll get it soon enough. Where were they hiding out?" She told him. "I wouldn't have thought of that place. The old hotel has been…you know, that explains a few things. A few days ago, a couple of the cubs from the leap told their parents that the hotel out there is haunted. That place has been empty for at least a few decades. We should maybe have it torn down. It's a sore sight anyway."

Carrie was speaking to what he assumed was the teenagers, telling them once again that they were dead and that dead was forever. She looked so frustrated that he wanted to help her but he didn't know what to say that she'd not. It was the kid's fault and that of their parents, the fact that they were dead. Who in their right mind would give a bunch of sixteen and seventeen-year-olds liquor when they could barely pump gasoline into their car. He's always heard the saying that people can get a hunting license by taking a test. Why didn't they have to take one to be a parent? The world was going crazy.

On their way home, both of them having been all over the town several times today working, he was able to meet up with a few of his jags to see if they would mind very much helping out the police department. He had ten volunteers and three more that offered to end his life before he made it. Archie was hard-pressed to tell them no, that he had to go to prison when he heard how much Douglas had upset his wife.

They were cooking out after the meeting. After telling Larry what he had for him, the man was grateful. He and Carrie sat in the living room, neither of them speaking just sitting back with their eyes closed to rest. He thought that he could stay like this forever, but there were things that he had to get finished up before he thought he'd have time to go to bed. It was sad when he had to schedule his bedtime nowadays. He wasn't at all happy with the way their personal life kept getting put on the back burner when they needed time off. When his brother, Weston, showed up at their home the next morning, neither he nor Carrie were in the best of moods. Weston seemed to understand and was willing to help them out.

"I found a place for the two of you to go for a week. It's actually one of your places that Dad had purchased. As it's a rental, all I had to do was not renew their lease agreement and have someone go in and have the place cleaned up so that the two of you can use it. As a matter of fact, when you guys return, Nash and Sunny are going to go there too. It's a very nice home. Staff will be there all the time and there is no phone service nor internet." Carrie said that it sounded too perfect. "It is, actually. While you're there, I only need one thing from you. There are a couple of buildings there that, as a family, we should buy. It's a port that we can use to bring in produce and take out what they're going to be selling. There are nine people, a family that are all willing to work in the warehouse if we help them sell their wool. They raise goats there."

"How have they been selling it before?" Weston told them. "So they had ships going out, but they're undependable. I can see that. Getting their products to the market would be a timed item. How much do you think the buildings will go for?"

As he and his brother worked out the arrangements on the buildings, Carrie was taking notes. She'd always been good at keeping him on track by doing that, and this time was no different. Once Weston had all the details worked out, he gave them tickets on the next flight out and gave them the information on the house. Archie was almost too excited because he was waiting for the other shoe to be dropped, and it did not happen. That was how things were going now for days and neither one of them was able to rest. Even when they went to bed, one or both of them were sound asleep before the other was. It was terrible.

It took them most of the next day and into the evening to work out the things that needed to be done to leave. A passport was needed for him as Carrie already had one. Since he'd never been out of the state much less the country, he was lacking a great many things that were needed to travel out of the country. That alone should have made him happy, but he was continually waiting for something to pull the rug out from under his feet and tell him that he wasn't going. Right up until they were boarded on the plane did Archie feel like they might be taking a much-needed vacation.

The plane landed in what he could only think of was paradise. There were palm trees all around the airport. Colorful homes and buildings all around the little place they'd landed. Even as far as he could see, which was far by his guesstimates, there were clear blue skies and sand. Even in the little building next to the airport where people picked up their luggage, there were tropical plants and beautiful paintings, as well as sand all over the floor, where it was swept in by the wonderful breeze that seemed to keep everyone and everything cool. They decided to stop off at one of the little cantinas to have a few appetizers as well as a glass of wine before heading to the house. He couldn't believe that the two of them were finally here, even though it had only been a few days since he'd learned about it. Archie decided that he was going to show his beautiful wife the best time that he could, without thought to ghosts, leaps or things going on at home.

There was a limo to pick them up when they were finished. Weston had arranged for them to have the same driver for the rest of their stay. Also, in the limo with them, there were maps of the island they were on as well as places that he'd made them reservations at so that they could enjoy the local cuisine. They were going to do just that, too. Enjoy the fuck out of the place.

By the time they were about to pull up in front of the house, he was having doubts again. Things were going just too well for him to believe everything he'd been told about the house. Almost as soon as they were in the drive, he knew that his brother had been wrong about the house. It was much nicer and larger than he'd said. It looked like it could hold a large family, with children too, and not have to overwork the household. Christ, the thing looked like it had been the island built around it. It was that perfect.

"Let's tour the grounds before we go in." Archie would do anything for Carrie, and even though he wanted to make sure that the bedroom they were staying in at least had a bed—he really needed to get out of the Danny-downer mood, they were shown the back deck and the sea that came right up to the steps to the boat dock. "Oh, Archie, this is perfect. Look how far you can see across the water."

They ate their dinner of seafood and fresh fruits in the little screened patio that was near the water. The breeze kept them cooled off, and the smells coming from the flowers that surrounded their yard were enough to make them both heady. Archie, new to having things go right for a change, didn't let the rest of the evening get tangled up in his thoughts. He was here to have a good time with his mate and damn the things going on around him.

Chapter 8

"When he makes it to the prison, he'll be put into solitary confinement as soon as he arrives. He'll spend the next fifty or so years there, only having time out of his cell for one hour a day in thirty-minute time slots where he can go outside. He will never have contact with another person for his life stay. Even his meals, which will be given to him through an opening that can only be accessed when there is a tray—there is a chip on the trays that he gets—in it will be his only way to be fed. If at any time he doesn't return the tray, he will not receive another tray with food until such time as he does." Wrangler asked how he was supposed to be let out into the open yard. "Through a door that is locked on the outside by a hinge and locking system. I'm proud to say that no one has ever gotten back out into the yard nor into the cell unless we're aware of it."

Wrangler watched the mechanism as they worked it. He had been sent here by Nash to make sure that there wasn't going to be any kind of escape made by Douglas. The man wouldn't be allowed any visitors for the first five years due to his record, nor would anyone speak to him on the inside. If he was ever ill, then he'd be drugged, and a doctor would see him while he was out. While Wrangler could see all kinds of things that could go wrong with that, they seemed to have a good backup plan in place so that he'd not be able to get out. All his toiletries, as well as mattresses and blankets, would be changed out when he was in the yard when necessary. Also, the shower was right in the cell with him so there was no need for him to leave the area even for that. Any personal items, candy bars, or whatever were added to his cell while he was out in the yard when they arrived for him.

It sounded like they had this the way that it should have been. All locked up and made so that their prisoners couldn't get out, nor could they interact with others and be able to do them harm. There was no doubt in anyone's mind that Douglass would kill anyone that got close to him. Douglas was a horrific person, and he wasn't going to change just because he was in prison. Wrangler was still at the prison when Douglas was brought in.

Wrangler was about as tense as he'd ever been, even being around his own mother. The jaguars that had helped put him into the van that brought him here were helping again when he was taken into the prison. Even going so far as to follow him all the way down the hall to his new home.

Wrangler didn't envy him at all. He knew that if he had to be couped up all day like that, he'd go insane. Douglas was smiling the entire time, like he had a big secret that he was keeping that would, somehow get him out. He'd gladly kill the man just to make sure that Carrie was safe from him. The man was a monster, and there was no denying that he'd come after Carrie if given the chance. He didn't understand how someone could hate so harshly. His mother and grandfather had been the same. He began to wonder if there were more people like them in the world. It was sad if that was true.

Once he was locked in his cell, Douglas tried all the doors. He had a moment of fear when he jerked on the door to the cell, and it moved. The guard with him laughed, saying that it was like that so they'd have a little false hope. He thought it was great, diabolical, but fun nonetheless.

After he laid down on his hard steel bed, just a sheet of metal that had been soldered to the wall, with a thin mattress, Wrangler left. As far as he was concerned, Douglas was no longer a threat to his family. If he ever got out, any or all of them would kill him where he stood. His thoughts were that the man should have been killed a long time ago. There would certainly be a lot less deaths because of him being free.

On his way home, he stopped to get some breakfast. The guard that had been showing him around had told him that *Little Drop of Happiness* had the best pancakes in the world. Wrangler took it as a challenge to go and see if he was right.

As soon as he was seated, he looked over the menu and decided that he was going to have the pancake special. It was five pancakes, three strips of bacon, two eggs, sausage, and coffee. He didn't drink coffee, so he was glad that he was able to substitute it out for tea. Not his favorite either but he could drink it more than he could the other stuff.

He was just cutting into the fluffiest pancakes he'd ever seen when the waitress, her name tag said her name was Mel, put a note on the table. When he started to ask her what was going on, but she cut him off and started talking about how she'd bring by his bill to him in a minute. To take his time. Thinking her odd, he waited until she refilled his little water pot of hot water before he read the note.

"Kitchen. At gunpoint. Help us. Please."

Standing up, he asked where the bathroom was, and that he'd be back. She pointed to the door that was right next to the kitchen door where she'd been coming out of and made his way there. Only he didn't enter the bathroom but let his cat take him and was happy when she pushed open the door to the kitchen for him.

It was then that it occurred to him that she was a cat, too, however, she was a lion. Being closer to the floor as his cat, he noticed that she not only had a chain of metal around her wrist but her ankle as well. This would prevent her from shifting. If she did, she'd lose not only her wrist but her ankle as well. More than likely bleeding out in the process. Whoever was robbing the place had done their homework to know what to expect, except for him. He was the odd man out today.

Making his way into the kitchen as quietly as he could, he could smell fresh blood. Seeing another waitress sitting on the floor with the same chains on her, she pointed to her left, telling him he supposed that someone was in that direction. He made his way there, but she stopped him before he could step around her.

When she put out her hand, it was shaking. Thinking that she wanted him to bite her for a connection, he put his mouth over her hand and waited. At her nod, he licked the area before biting down on her soft hand. She didn't make a sound but nodded when he closed the wound.

"The rest of the staff is in the cooler, with the exception of the manager. The others have been in there a long time, and I'm worried that they will die. Can you hurry this along so that I can get them out?" He told her that he'd do his best and asked her how many people were in the place. *"There are eight of us that*

work here. Four employees in the cooler, the manager, cook, me and Mel. Then, there are four men with guns. They're waiting for the morning rush so that they can get more money. I don't know what they think is going to happen to them. Every one of the morning rush is police officers and guards from the prison. You're the first regular person that has been in here in months."

It didn't take him very long to take the man holding a gun to what he assumed was the chef out. Tearing his throat out, the man was long dead before he hit the floor. The man was so grateful that he bowed at him, then grabbed up the other waitress and left the kitchen area.

Moving to the other end of the kitchen, Wrangler encountered two more men and killed them both as well. There was only one more that he'd have to deal with, and he had to ask the young woman where he might be. She told him that he was sitting at the manager's desk, holding her on his lap with a gun to her head as he fondled her.

Entering the smallish room, snarling at the man, he stood up and fired six times in his general direction, missing him every time. The last two shots hit him in the chest when he stood up to kill the man. Slicing his paw across his throat, he dispatched the man quickly before he passed out.

The woman had been tossed to the floor, where she hit her head. It was bleeding, so he licked the wound closed and made his way to the bathroom to shift again. He knew that he couldn't die, but the pain of being shot and so close hurt like hell. He was never so thankful for Sunny and her magic as he was right then.

Mel had called the police while he'd been in the bathroom and knew that they'd be slightly jumpy — he would if it was him — when they came into their favorite place to eat with four dead men and a stranger there.

Wrangler laid his gun on the table he'd been seated at with his permit to carry along side of it. Sunny and her mother Lily had arrived too, making sure that the bodies of the men were 'shot' and not had their throats ripped out when viewed by the police and anyone else that had to deal with them. The others, the staff that had been sequestered in the cooler, were now in the dining area with the others. Everyone knew their part to play when the first officer showed up.

By then, not only was Wrangler sitting on the floor, he had his fingers laced behind his head, his pockets were turned out and he had opened his shirt so that they could see that he wasn't carrying anything else with him. They were polite, if not a little jumpy as he'd thought they would be, but after a bit, they allowed him to get up and straighten out his clothing. He sat back down to eat the rest of his cold breakfast.

"Did you know these men?" He told the officer that he'd only stopped by here on the way home at the recommendation of one of the guards. He nodded. "We come here every day. It's a nice little place. I want to thank you for helping out my mom. She's Mel Sharpley, the owner of this place."

He told the other man that she'd been smart in handing him a note to warn him. Officer Sharpley said that sounded like something that she'd do. Smiling at him, the man sat across from him before looking around at the other officers.

"She is going to close this place up soon. This might just be the final straw for her. I hate to see it go. I've spent my entire life here at some point or another." Wrangler asked him what he'd like for him to do. "You're that Sheppard family. The ones that help out people that are in need, right? Well, I'd like to apply for help for my mom. She won't get what she needs to live off of, and being in her seventies, she'll hopefully be around for a bit longer. People want a cheap deal because they figure that she's old and doesn't have a brain cell one. But she's savvy. Will you lend her the money to fix this place up so that she can resell it at a better price? I don't know all the ends and outs of what might be needed nor the cost of such things. But I do know that whatever is needed, it will make a world of difference for the rest of her life. I'd make sure that you're paid back from the proceeds of the sale. She just needs a helping hand."

"Yes. I'll loan her the money." Wrangler surprised himself with his quick answer. It wasn't like him to not think things over for days before still not having a solid answer. "I'll hire someone to come in and tell us what it would cost to do the renovations. Also, to tell us if it would be worth doing. That would be something that you'd have to think about, too. The place might have structural things wrong with it that we can't see right now." Billy, as he was asked to call him, said he'd thought of that too. "Good. You're a good son. What is your mom going to think about going behind her back and doing this?"

"She'll smack me in the back of the head, then tell me that she loves me for helping her. I'd just like for her to have enough money to buy food for herself and a roof over her head. Right now, do you think that will be possible?" He didn't want to commit to something that he had no knowledge of but said that he thought so. Again, something that he'd never done before. "Thank you for being honest with me, Wrangler. You've no idea how much I appreciate this."

"It's no problem. But don't be thanking me just yet. This might be all for nothing." He told him that he understood that, too. "You're a good son, Billy. Looking after your mother shows me too that you're not in this for yourself. Thank you for restoring my faith in humanity today."

After the police left and he was given a platter of food on the house, he left his business card with Billy and headed home. Excited to have a new venture to invest in, he started making calls as soon as he got home. It just so happened that one of the men in the leap that his brother ran was a construction company owner. He was more than willing to go out and check on the place.

~*~

Archie didn't want to go home. Tomorrow was their last day here, and they'd had such a wonderful time that he considered just saying fuck it all and live here forever. But he also knew that the two of them had obligations that they just couldn't walk away from. However, he thought knowing that they could come here and spend some down time when it got to be too much he thought would make leaving a great deal easier.

They'd walked the island so many times that he was sure that he could do it with his eyes closed. The two of them had tried so many different kinds of foods, things that he'd only read about when he'd been escaping through the words in a book. The colors were so vibrant that he couldn't imagine not having them around all the time.

Carrie had been napping during the day. He was sure that she was worn out from all the lovemaking that they'd been having. Just yesterday, she woke him up riding his cock so beautifully that he'd nearly forgotten that he could enjoy their lovemaking too. Christ, the places where they'd had quick sex boggled his mind that they'd not been caught a few times that it was very close. And each time, the two of them would come so hard that they would have to rest for an hour or two before being able to walk without staggering. It was the best fun he'd had, he thought.

Now, here they were in the big bed for the last time this vacation. Carrie was sleeping, and he was just dozing off when he remembered that he'd not set an alarm. Pulling his phone to him, he set his clock to wake up in plenty of time to get dressed, packed, and go to the airport the next morning. Closing his eyes, he fell into a deep sleep.

Waking up, his cock warm and wet, he looked down at his body in the moonlight to see Carrie sucking his cock. Reaching for the light so he could watch her enjoying herself, he knocked off not just his phone but the little glass of water that he had there nightly. Once the light was on, he nearly came watching her lick along the crown of his cock. She smiled at him even as she cupped his balls gently in her hands and fondled them lightly.

"I want you to come all over me." He nodded, not sure that he could form any kind of coherent words to convey anything. "I want to feel your cum all over me so that I can rub it into my skin."

"Yes." He reached down to his cock, fisting

it in his hand as she sat up over him. He wanted to
toss her over onto the bed and take her hard, but
he also wanted her to have what she wanted. As
soon as his balls began to fill painfully, he told her
that he was coming. It started at the top of his head
and raced down to his cock as he exploded.

He watched as his cum hit her body. Her
breasts were covered in long drips of his cum
that made him dizzy with the need to give her
more. When she rubbed it into her skin, making
her nipples hard, he came again, hurting a bit but
enjoying his mate as she licked his cum off her
hands and then rubbed it into her mouth. Coming
again, three times in a row, was a record for them,
but he was sure that if she were to touch him right
now, he'd simply pass out. His body was tense
with his need to fill her that he finally grabbed
her body, rolled over, and slammed his cock deep
inside of her wet heat.

They both cried out. He held her body to his
as he emptied over and over into her. Dropping
atop of her, it was all he could do to breathe. There
wasn't going to be any moving by him in the next
year or so. Laughing a little, he did manage to flop
over, his body half in and out of the bed. But he

wasn't crushing her, so he thought that he could live with that for now.

The next time that he woke up, the alarm screaming at him from across the room for some reason, he got up and stepped in the glass, managing to cut his foot open and had him cursing up a storm. Grabbing his phone, he dropped it again, shattering the screen and breaking his case as well.

Turning when he heard laughter, he watched as Carrie was rolling in the bed, laughing hard at him while trying to talk that he found himself laughing with her. It had been a hell of a morning so far, and they'd not even left the house.

After hurrying through their packing, him shifting to take care of his foot, they decided to have their luggage, more than what they came with taken to the airport and have lunch one more time at their favorite place. He'd grown very fond of lobster sandwiches and was going to have to find out if the cook could make them for him at home. Also, grilled pineapple. He had never tried it before at home now he couldn't get enough of it.

"I'm going to head to the bathroom. Did you want some dessert? I would love a mango smoothie." When she left, the waiter came to take away the dishes, and he asked for two of the desserts that Carrie had wanted. But he got them to go. They really needed to get going if they were going to get to the airport on time. When she came out, they took their drinks and headed to the car.

"I don't want to leave. We've made so many memories here that I just want to stay here forever." He told the love of his life that he didn't either. That he'd enjoyed this so much. "We'll be back, right? I mean, it would be nice to be able to think about having another vacation here. Now that we've settled up on the building that your brother wanted us to look into, someone will have to come down on occasion to make sure that things are going well here."

"Yes. But it might not always be you and I." She pouted at him, and he laughed a little. "I have enjoyed this so much and all because of you. You are my reason to live, my heart to beat and making me a better man. I cannot tell you enough just how much I love you."

"I love you as well, Archie. So much." They got to the airport in time to get themselves something to drink on the ride home.

Archie decided that he wanted to bring a little of the place that they'd had so much fun at to their home so while waiting on the drinks, he wandered into a gift shop and found a cookbook on the local cuisine. He was looking through the pages, thinking that it had just the things that he'd wanted in it, when someone brushed up against him while standing still.

While not really thinking about it, he did turn to look at the person. He looked to be about ten years old and malnourished. He was sure that the kid had tried to pickpocket his wallet, but Archie had it in his breast pocket, having been told that there were a lot of undesirable sorts around the area.

"Mister? You have any change? I've not been able to eat for a few days." He asked him where his parents were. "I can't go back there. They're planning to sell me and my sister off. She's got herself a job now but she doesn't get paid for a few more days. We're about starved."

For whatever reason, he believed the kid. Pulling out the money that he had in his pocket, he handed it over to the kid. It was about forty dollars, and when he took the five and tried to hand the rest back to him, Archie told him to keep it. To get his sister a meal, too. He wrapped his arms around him.

The boy was shaking. He was crying so hard. He kept thanking him for the money and that he'd pay him back. He didn't know how that was going to work but didn't say anything to the boy. After he seemed to have a handle on his emotions, he stepped back and put out his hand. The connection to the kid was immediate and he knew then that the kid had been telling the truth about not just him starving but about his parents as well.

Paying for the cookbook, he held onto the kid until they were out of the shop. The woman at the counter didn't look happy about having the boy in her place, but she didn't say anything other than what he owed on the cookbook. Hurrying out of the shop, he found Carrie just where he'd left her. Telling her briefly what had happened, he asked the boy for his name.

"William Damon. My sister calls me Wills. My parents called me Shit for Brains." He asked about his sister. "She's on the cleaning crew here. Cleaning up after people when they get on the planes. People sure do leave a lot of crap behind when they leave, don't they?"

"I agree. The beaches here are a prime example of that happening, too. Can you locate your sister? I have an idea that the two of you are in deeper with your parents than you told me." Wills lowered his head and said that they were. That they'd been hiding from them for a while now. "Get your sister, Wills, and we'll make arrangements for you to come home with us. You'll be safe there."

"Just like that. You're going to take my word for all this?" He asked him if he was lying to him. "No. Amber told me that if you start lying, it'll catch up with you sooner than later and that it's hard to keep track of what you say so it'll give you a heart attack trying to keep it all straight. It's just easier to tell the truth."

"Your sister sounds like a brilliant woman." Wills said that he could find her, and Carrie said she'd go with him. Archie went to the front desk, purchased two more tickets and was thrilled to no end that it worked out that there was enough room on the plane.

He had a moment of wonder. Like Wills, he wondered why he was doing this for strangers.

He'd seen in the kid's mind when they connected that their parents had beaten the two of them just recently, and it was only now that his sister, Amber, had been able to get up and around enough to work. Wills was too young, of course, but he would keep an eye on his sister when he could so she'd not be found by them. He just could not understand people nowadays. They all seemed to be a bit or more at times like his own mother had been.

Amber was coming toward them with Carrie and Wills. The young woman had a backpack in her hands, and Archie knew instinctively that she couldn't wear it on her back because of the beating she'd recently had. As soon as the introductions were made, the three of them sat in the airport lobby while he went to get them some food and drink. Wills came with him.

"You don't have to do this, mister." He told him to call him Archie. "All right, Archie. We can get by on the money you already gave me for a few days. Amber is getting better, and we've found us a good place to hide at night."

"My brothers, I have five of them, would murder me if I didn't help you out. That's something that we've decided to do for anyone who needed it. Was to help out people that have been hurt by the very people that were supposed to love them." He handed him three subs and asked him to pick out some chips that his sister would like. "You'll be far enough away from them that they won't be able to hurt you. And if they end up finding you, they'll never harm you again. You have my word on that."

When Wills agreed that he'd take the food to his sister, Archie picked up a couple of fruit cups along with several bottles of water. While they had asked for water to drink, he didn't know that either one of them would turn down some more of it. As soon as he sat back with his little family, he handed out the things that he had and noticed that one of the subs was already gone. Good, they weren't shy about eating when someone offered it to them.

When their flight was called, the four of them got up to stand in line. He could feel the exact moment that Amber was stressed out and turned to ask her what was happening. Apparently, their parents had figured out that they were staying at the airport.

Calling to Sunny to help them out, it was her mom that showed up. Lily was dressed like the people in line with them, but she glowed with magic. Just putting her hands on Amber and Wills, she asked them both to stand very still. Archie let out a huge breath, with the older couple walked right by them without noticing the kids.

"My name is Lily. I've been keeping an eye on the two of you for a bit now. You've done so much for my earth every day by picking up things left behind that I wish to reward you." She looked at Amber. "You're in a great deal of pain. I can almost taste it on you. How about I fix that up for you and your brother?"

She didn't wait for an answer but touched her hands to their face. Amber was shocked, he could see that but it was Wills that seemed to be the happiest. Not knowing how he had been hurting, he was glad to see that the young boy was smiling. Then, what Lily had said occurred to him.

"Is Amber going to be a part of my family?" She just smiled at him, and he grinned back. *"Oh, this is going to be epic. Which one?"*

"I shant tell you. You're much too eager to have entirely too much fun with this. They'll be safe with

the family, and that is a great deal more important than anything else right now." He agreed with her. Archie didn't like it but he did agree. The queen of the earth looked at their new family members. "All right. The four of you will be safe but you're to keep an eye out for traps. The couple will stop at nothing to get you two back."

"Yes, all right. And thank you for taking the pain away. I was sick with it." Lily told Amber that it had been her pleasure. "I don't know how to thank you, too, for keeping us safe. It's been a very long time since anyone has shown any kind of compassion to either of us. Now we have had it twice in one day. Thank you all."

When they were seated on the plane, he was glad now that he'd purchased the last two seats in first class. They were the first to board, and they'd be the first to disembark. While the flight wasn't long, Wills must have been exhausted as he fell asleep almost as soon as they were allowed to take their seatbelts off. He did notice that neither one of the sister and brother duo did that so he was content to let them sleep until they landed.

Archie hoped that all his family was present when they got to the airport. He wanted this meeting between whoever was her mate to happen quickly. Archie only wanted the best for his family and honestly didn't care which one of them would find a mate in Amber. He wondered too if whichever brother it was, they'd be fine with taking on Wills too. If not, he'd have a place with them. He had enjoyed talking with the boy and thought that he'd fit right in with the rest of the family.

Leaning back, Carrie laid her head on his chest and closed her eyes. Archie wasn't tired, but he was happy to be able to watch over his little family while they did sleep. Christ, he thought, who would have thought that their wonderful vacation could end on such a note as having brought more family with them. Smiling, he was glad that he was going back now. But in a few days, he knew that he'd wish they were back on the island.

Before You Go...

HELP AN AUTHOR

write a review

THANK YOU!

Share your voice and help guide other readers to these wonderful books. Even if it's only a line or two, your reviews help readers discover the author's books so they can continue creating stories that you'll love. Log in to your favorite retailer and leave a review. Thank you.

AWARD WINNING, BESTSELLING AUTHOR

Kathi Barton, a winner of the Pinnacle Book Achievement Award and a best-selling author on Amazon and All Romance books, lives in Nashport, Ohio, with her husband, Paul. When not creating new worlds and romance, Kathi and her husband enjoy camping and going to auctions. She can also be seen at county fairs with her husband, an artist and potter.

Her muse, a cross between Jimmy Stewart and Hugh Jackman, brings her stories to life for her readers in a way that has them coming back time and again for more. Her favorite genre is paranormal romance, with a great deal of spice. You can visit Kathi online and drop her an email if you'd like. She loves hearing from her fans. aaronskiss@gmail.com.

Follow Kathi on her blog: http://kathisbartonauthor.blogspot.com/

www.ingramcontent.com/pod-product-compliance
Lightning Source LLC
Chambersburg PA
CBHW032004170626
46807CB00006B/2647